To Alisdair
Enjoy the read

THE SHADOW MEN

Alan Evans

MINERVA PRESS
LONDON
ATLANTA MONTREUX SYDNEY

ISBN 1 86106 830 1

First Published 1998 by
MINERVA PRESS
195 Knightsbridge
London SW7 1RE

Printed in Great Britain for Minerva Press

THE SHADOW MEN

This book is dedicated to the memory of
John Ronald Evans
(1953–1985)

Contents

Chapter One
Down but not Out

'The Home Office guidelines for this offence is fourteen years to life. However, you have a young family – eleven years. Take him down.'

The silence of the courtroom was only broken by a muffled sob from his wife; he glanced around the room, taking in the faces to be imprinted on his mind like an old photograph. The screw that was in the dock with him beckoned for him to move; he ignored him for a moment as he caught his wife's eye.

She mouthed, 'I love you,' silently across the quiet room.

He blew her a kiss and pointed for her to come down to the cells under the court. The quietness now broken with the clatter of movement on the dock's wooden floor, he looked around once more before he took the final steps to the stairway leading down to the cold empty cells deep in the bowels of this modern-day incarceration pit. It was only minutes later when the door opened again, although it felt like hours. A strange woman entered his cell; he looked through her, expecting to see his wife following behind, but there were only two screws hovering in the background. The woman spoke softly, saying that she was a probation officer and that she had spoken to his wife outside but unfortunately 'they', whoever 'they' were, would not let her visit him in the cells; they had told her that he would be going back to Brixton Prison and that she should visit him there the following day.

'She said to tell you that she loves you and she will wait however long it takes,' said the probation woman.

'We'll see,' he mumbled, still in shock at the sentence.

They took him from the court to Wandsworth Prison, with his wife now looking forward to seeing him the following day at Brixton. Having never even heard of Wandsworth she would be confused to say the least.

He took note of the screw's sick sense of humour and rightly so as this was to be the first of many such incidents.

He had already spent almost a year in custody on remand at Wormwood Scrubs Prison in London then a week at Brixton Prison while on trial; now he was in Wandsworth Prison, another Victorian prison, all of them with little or no sanitation.

He was in shock not just at the sentence but at the state of the prison system – the fact that it was 1989 and there he was in a cell with no access to a toilet or a shower or even to clean underwear.

At Wandsworth there was only a plastic bucket with a lid for use as a toilet, though most only used this to urinate in to. If they needed to crap they would do it on paper or into an old carrier bag then throw it out of the window so as to avoid the stench of it in the bucket all night, which could be quite annoying to the other people sharing the same cell – in Wandsworth many of the cells housed two, three and in some cases even four men to a cell.

Jack was lucky in that way he was a category 'A' prisoner so he was in a cell on his own, but even that couldn't get him more than one pair of semi-clean underpants at the weekly shower and kit change ritual.

After many months of the tortures of Wandsworth, Jack was stopped on the landing and told to report to the allocation office. He went along to the office with the hope of a move to a more tolerable prison; waiting outside in the queue until it was his turn to go in, he watched the faces of the people coming out of the office, some looking joyous, some in despair, depending on where they were being sent to.

'Next!' a voice boomed from the other side of the door.

Jack walked in and waited.

'What's your name and number?' the screw scowled.

'Dunkerley PXX 499,' said Jack while thinking, 'if I ever met this big-mouthed shitbag outside of this wall I'd willingly alter his walking arrangements.'

'Right Dunkerley, you are being transferred tomorrow to Parkhurst prison on the Isle of Wight; have you anything to say?'

'Well yes, as a matter of fact I have,' said Jack. 'For a start I live in the north of England and you're sending me even further south – it's difficult enough for my family to visit me as it is.'

'Well it's not up to us, Dunkerley, you are a Cat 'A' prisoner and you have to go where the Home Office sends you.'

'So that's the end of that, then,' said Jack.

'Looks that way doesn't it, Dunkerley?' said the screw and on that note Jack left and wandered back to his cell.

The next morning Jack was up early feeling a bit anxious and apprehensive about what the next few hours would bring.

He packed the hundreds of letters from his wife along with the many phone numbers he had collected from other inmates (whom he hoped would prove useful one day) and what few belongings he had accumulated over the previous two years into a couple of battered boxes and then, until his door was unlocked, he lay on top of the mattress waiting and thinking.

He thought mainly about what was to lie ahead of him and of all the violence and bad things that he had heard of at Parkhurst prison over the last couple of years. Jack was surprised when he got onto the prison van; as a Cat 'A' prisoner he was usually moved from prison to prison alone; however, this time there were other prisoners on the front part of the bus. Jack was moved along maybe three-quarters of the way back – there were already three screws sitting along the back row. Jack, who was already handcuffed, had one side of the handcuffs undone and the manacle was then attached to a chain that ran from the front of the bus to the back underneath the seats.

Jack was not impressed with this form of transport. He thought about the worst scenario – an accident. What would happen if the bloody thing caught fire? Or, just as bad, what if something happened to the ferry on the forty-minute crossing from the mainland to the island!

Although Jack felt that he was a competent swimmer, two things bothered him, one being that the Solent was one of the most treacherous stretches of water in the world and, two, that being chained to a two-ton van might create havoc with his breast stroke. He was not happy with either of these possibilities.

The crossing was windy and uncomfortable and Jack could feel a light sweat across his brow; he felt a sigh of relief as the ferry docked but he was still anxious about the fate that awaited him at Parkhurst.

The first sighting of Parkhurst as he approached the prison shattered his preconceptions. This was not as he had imagined it to be at all, his illusion thankfully destroyed. This was not Britain's answer to America's Alcatraz, an ancient monument perched on a rock protruding from the sea, continually battered by the cold sea and wind. No, this was a modern prison, at least on the outside. The new wall with the domed top and the new electronic gatehouse, the mass of security cameras, all this technology and modernity completely threw Jack who had approached the island with a feeling of impending doom. He was soon dealt with in the reception area and with a politeness he was unaccustomed to, especially by screws – was this some sort of head game? Jack wondered if this was something along the line of good cop, bad cop. 'Hmm, we'll soon see,' he supposed.

One of the screws said, 'Pick up your property and follow me, Mr Dunkerley.'

Mr, thought Jack. This is some kind of wind-up after the abuse he'd got used to in the Victorian prisons of London, where the screws are viewed as failed gas meter readers with a collective IQ that doesn't reach double figures.

Jack picked up his belongings and followed the screw through gate after gate, waiting at each one for it to be opened and then locked again behind them with that ever-familiar sound of a heavy clang, which would always send a shiver down Jack's spine, the clang that would live with him for ever and be the waking noise of a thousand nightmares. Before they had reached 'B' wing Jack had to stop and put his boxes down; he was out of breath.

'How much further now, boss?' said Jack.

'We're about halfway there,' the screw replied.

'Bloody hell,' said Jack. 'I'm knackered, I've not done this much work for two years. I've done nothing but lay on my bed reading and eating, that's why I've put so much fat on I reckon, especially with the prison stodge that we get.'

The screw laughed. 'Yes I've seen it,' he said. 'There's a gym here so you'll soon get a few pounds off – if you make use of it.'

Not a bad idea, Jack thought as he picked up his stuff and continued his walk to find his new home. When they arrived at 'B' wing the place was deserted. Everyone must be at work or banged up, he thought.

Jack looked around and thought the outside of the prison had given such a modern view but the interior was no different than the Victorian institutions of London. This place was just as dirty and unkempt as the last.

Jack was called into an office on the ground floor. He walked in and shut the door. The screw said, 'Don't leave your stuff out there, mate, or it'll go on the missing list.'

Just my bloody luck, thought Jack. 'I've only been here an hour and already I'm a potential robbery victim, and why is this screw calling me mate? He's not my mate, is he? Very odd.'

Jack dragged his boxes into the screw's office with him.

'Just a few questions then we'll find you a cell. You are PXX 499 J. Dunkerley?'

'That's correct,' said Jack. He'd heard all these questions a thousand times before on his tour of London's prisons.

Jack had that cold feeling down his backbone, that feeling that you get when someone walks over your grave, the feeling that told him to be aware, but there was only him and one screw in the office and he was nothing to fear.

Jack turned and looked out of the window in the office door and there was the biggest man he'd seen in his life – he must have been twenty-five to thirty stone and was as black as coal. He just stood there staring, not saying a word. Jack turned to the screw and said, 'They're not all that size, are they?'

The screw grinned a little then turned back to his paperwork.

'You are in cell number twenty-one on the threes, which is really the twos as this is not the ground floor but the twos the ones which people think this is, is actually underneath this floor and in effect is the block.'

'Amazing,' said a bewildered Jack.

He collected his belongings and wandered off to find number twenty-one on the threes, the screw following a while later to open the door.

'What happens now?' asked Jack.

'Not a lot,' said the screw as he walked off.

'Don't you lock the door?' said Jack.

'Not at this time of the day,' said the screw. 'Have a look around, clean out your cell or take a shower.'

Then he disappeared onto another landing.

Jack stood inside his new home, another Victorian cell with no sanitation and only a small window for air. Not very pleasant, he thought, but it's all I've got, so I'll have to make the best of it.

He found a brush and cleaned out the cell before taking a shower.

Later he stood on the landing just looking around when the silence was broken by a sudden burst of activity – the other inmates were returning from the workshops and the education department.

Jack looked around at the new faces and even recognised a few from previous establishments. About twenty minutes later Jack noticed amongst the activity that many of the men were carrying plastic plates and cups. 'Obviously dinner time,' thought Jack. 'I'm feeling a bit peckish after today's events – I may as well join them.'

Jack collected his utensils from his cell and wandered down to the twos landing to join the queue.

After tea Jack wandered about for a while trying to find his way around, looking out for where the toilets were and finding a cell on each landing that had been converted into a kitchen for the inmates to cook their own food.

There was also a little room on each landing with a TV inside.

Jack sat down to watch the television – he hadn't seen one for a while. It had been over an hour since tea and Jack was settling down to watch the news when all of a sudden there was this mighty ringing around the jail like a fire bell; a couple of people got up to go and see what was happening but most of them didn't stir.

Jack gave it a few minutes then casually walked out onto the landing; people were looking down to the ground floor.

Jack looked down and there to his amazement was the thirty stone black guy he'd seen earlier, laid out on the floor. Apparently he had been stabbed sixteen times.

Jack never saw or heard of him again.

As in all the other prisons Jack had been to, he spoke to many prisoners, making friends with some and taking care to avoid others, always with an eye to the future and his master plan taking time and effort to meet and talk with what he thought were the right people to know.

There was no rush for Jack – he still had many years left to go in the system.

He had seen the so-called gangsters with their designer tracksuits and trainers; these high-profile people would never fit in with Jack's plan.

He had also seen hard drug users who denied ever touching the stuff while continuing to destroy their very souls; the few who would admit it would always have an excuse for doing so – 'it takes away the pain,' they'd say.

What pain? thought Jack, not quite understanding what they meant.

Jack had also seen guys, big strong tough guys totally destroyed in body, soul and reputation. He knew that once a man started to chase the dragon, once he had used this drug, then it wouldn't be long before the drug began to use him, then he had nothing left. He had sold his soul to the devil and cheaply at that, now not even his word could be relied upon.

This brown demon was the continual source for many of the beatings, stabbings and burnings (with boiling water and sugar or boiling fat) – these were not one-off occurrences at Parkhurst, these were everyday events.

Jack's next door neighbour, Happy Harry, was a bit of a drug user, though not to the extent that most were. He was what was known colloquially as a pothead. Jack didn't even know that he used the stuff until he saw him sober one day.

Harry was a quite likeable chap, easygoing, no problem to converse with and never looking for trouble, and Jack liked that. He didn't want any trouble either, he just wanted to get through the sentence as quickly and quietly as possible; not that he was a coward either – he'd been a natural fighter as a child, always able to hold his own in a row.

He had taken up martial arts at the age of nine and started work as a nightclub bouncer in his late teens; he spent the next sixteen years in this occupation until finally opening the first of his own two nightclubs in Manchester in the mid-eighties which he lost when he had all his assets seized after being found guilty at his trial.

That, however, was not the most important thing in the world to Jack; much more important were his wife and children, one child having been born after he was arrested. It tore him apart to be separated from them but there was no changing his current dilemma. At least his wife and children were still there for him so he had to get on with it and he had no choice in that.

Although Jack had been around a long time he still fell for sob stories at times and found himself out of pocket on several occasions.

He usually laughed at his own misfortune but on three occasions found himself in the firing line of trouble.

The first was caused by a mad Scotsman called MacDougall, though Jack never did find out what it was about. MacDougall ran into Jack's cell and poked Jack in the chest while shouting some incoherent abuse.

Jack was an easygoing, laid-back sort of guy and could take all kinds of verbal abuse but he lived on the understanding that when a guy puts his hands on you it was too late for talking and that made it show time.

Jack pushed MacDougall and MacDougall fell backwards against the cell wall. He looked up at Jack, his eyes ablaze with madness. Jack could see what he was thinking and said, 'Just get out of here.'

At this point MacDougall flew towards Jack, throwing wild punches. Jack waited for the right moment then let fly with a big right hander which crumpled MacDougall's face and sent him into a sort of acrobatic back flip.

'There's a screw coming!' someone shouted from outside the room. MacDougall, still glaring at Jack like a mad dog, headed out of the door and scurried off along the landing. He was taken out of the prison later that day to an outside hospital to have his cheekbone repaired.

He never came back for round two.

The next time that trouble came was when Jack had lent a hundred pounds to a guy in his mid-twenties, a guy called Grucker, from Gloucester. He told the story that he used to be a boxer and if nothing else he seemed to believe it himself.

The problem with this guy was that he turned out to be another junkie and was suffering from some sort of paranoia.

Jack had put no pressure on him at all but Grucker was getting worried that he had not paid back the debt, so worried in fact that he started to spread rumours that Jack was a grass. This was a typical cowardly way to get someone removed; however, he had not counted on the fact that Jack had been around the system for quite some time and was now quite well known, and Grucker could not make anyone believe such a story. He then resorted to putting notes in the screw's box saying that Jack was dealing in drugs.

Once again he was not believed.

In a final bid of desperation he stopped Jack on the landing and said,

'Can I have a word with you, Jack?'

'Not a problem,' said Jack not really expecting anything more than another sob story. Grucker went into Jack's cell and Jack followed.

Jack then turned to close the door and as he turned around to speak to Grucker, he caught a sudden movement from the corner of his eye.

Jack's years of experience working in the clubs as a bouncer suddenly came into their own; he sidestepped Grucker's first punch while releasing one of his own straight from the hip. It caught Grucker under the chin and lifted him off his feet and as he came crashing to the floor, Jack was there with a follow-up punch to the face which was like a pile driver, crushing Grucker's head between Jack's fist and the cell floor.

At this point Grucker took evasive action and rolled under Jack's bed, kicking over a bucket of urine in the process.

It was a sight for sore eyes – the floor covered in blood and piss and Grucker refusing to come out from under the bed at any price. Eventually Jack dragged Grucker out from under the bed and threw him out of the cell onto the landing.

Another one for the outside hospital with ingrowing cheekbones.

The third case of Jack fighting was when he lent another Scotsman sixty pounds. The Scotsman, named Bailey, had on one occasion tried to pay the money back, but it had gone missing in the post. This was a genuine mistake and Jack could understand that, but the scenario that followed was quite different in that Jack lent Bailey ten more pounds so that he could take the post office to a tribunal, which he did and which he won.

The post office returned the original sixty pounds plus the ten pounds costs. Bailey didn't know that Jack had been in the office when the envelope had arrived. Bailey then set about trying to con Jack saying that he hadn't had the money and was still waiting for it; a few days later Bailey went to Jack's cell with another sob story. By this time Jack had definitely had enough – Bailey was relying on the fact that Jack was an easygoing chap, an easy touch for a few quid, a bit gullible to a sob story, a bit of a big softie.

He picked the wrong day. Jack knocked him out.

Jack's mind wandered back to memories of yesteryear; he reminisced about such incidents that had happened to him and others since he was sentenced some four years ago. He had many memories which he looked upon as an education of life – he was going to learn from all his experiences.

Jack had come to Parkhurst as a Cat 'A' prisoner and, after being downgraded to a Cat 'B' last year, he was now on the verge of being downgraded once more to a Cat 'C'. To Jack that meant the possibility of a short home leave, out on a Friday morning and back by the following Monday evening.

Not long, thought Jack, but it certainly beats being in prison.

Four years, Jack mumbled, four long years.

It sounds like nothing if you say it fast but if you're doing the time in one of Her Majesty's hell-holes then you'll know each second, each minute, each hour and every day is like a never-ending torture and the only relief from Jack's pain and the monotony of prison life was the monthly visits from his wife Sandra and the rare visits from his children. One, the youngest, had problems with travelling and the older one could not continually have time away from school, so most of the monthly visits had been just Jack and Sandra.

Jack knew that he had a wife in a million; she had written almost daily since he was arrested and she had not missed any opportunity to visit him in all their years apart. It was a caring love that Jack had not given a second thought to before his arrest, but with time to ponder these things in the many hours of emptiness, Jack came to the conclusion that he had married the right woman. She had never let him down or complained about having to wait so long for her man to come home; she was happy in the knowledge that he would one day be coming home and it mattered not how long that would be.

'I'll have to write and tell her that there's the possibility of a home leave soon,' thought Jack, but at the same time he didn't want to build up her hopes only to have them dashed again at the last moment like so many times before.

Jack was awaiting his first parole review and thought to himself that he wouldn't have to worry about the home leave if he got a good result from the parole board. Some weeks passed before the parole answers came back and Jack did not get the answer that he was hoping for. So now it would be another year before he could try again.

Jack did however have his status to Cat 'C' granted and he immediately applied for his first home leave. It seemed to take for ever and in the few days before Jack was due to leave the prison for a short home leave, he was as excited as a child at Christmas. It would be his first time outside a prison wall in four extremely long years.

Jack walked out of the prison gates at 7.30 a.m. to be met by Sandra running towards him. She threw her arms around him and they kissed passionately; then with their arms around each other they walked to their car.

It was to be the first time that Jack had seen it. 'Would you like to drive, Jack?'

'Do you think I should, it's been a long time since I last drove.'

'You'll manage just fine,' said Sandra.

Jack got into the driving seat and adjusted the driving position.

'You'll have to give me some directions,' said Jack, laughing. 'I haven't a clue where we're going to.'

'We'll be okay,' she replied.

Jack started the engine but before driving off he turned to look at his wife; she was staring at him, smiling, her face now more alive than he had seen it for many years. She leaned towards him and they kissed with an intensity that was electric.

'Let's get back to the guest house,' said Jack.

They had to call there to collect his wife's travel bags before catching the ferry and heading home.

They parked outside the front door of the guest house and went inside.

Sandra introduced Jack to Mary, who was the owner. The two women had become good friends over the years, with Sandra having stayed there many times whilst visiting Jack. The woman's husband then entered the room.

'This is Roger, Mary's husband,' said Sandra.

Roger was a bit of a computer buff and rambled on in computer jargon most of the time, not noticing that he was mostly ignored.

Jack was computer-literate, having studied computers while in prison and having read many books on the subject whiling away the hours, but at this present moment in time computers were the last thing that he wanted to discuss. Jack was more interested in being alone with his wife and after repeated hints, winks and nods he went with his wife to collect her things from her room.

The door had hardly closed behind them when they threw their arms around each other and kissed with an unrivalled passion.

Jack picked Sandra up and carried her across the room to the bed. He laid her down on top of the quilt and then lay down beside her; they kissed and hugged each other for a while. Jack started to undress his wife with an urgency that only someone who had spent many years in prison could understand – the smell of a woman, the taste of a woman, the warmth of her touch... Jack had waited such a long time for this moment and now his dream would become a reality. He stripped her down to her bra and knickers, her milky white skin contrasting with her black underwear.

He kicked off his shoes and took off his socks. Sandra then unbuttoned his denim shirt and slipped it off his shoulders; Jack pushed the shirt off the bed and it fell to the floor, closely followed by the rest of his clothes.

He lay there completely naked and watched as his wife's eyes took in every inch of his body.

He sat her up on the bed put his arms around her and struggled to undo the fastener on her bra.

'I'm out of practice,' said Jack.

'I should hope so,' said Sandra.

Jack finally managed to undo the fastener and he slipped the bra straps off her shoulders, down along her arms then pulled it away from her body before throwing it across the room. Her breasts now laid bare before him, he caressed them gently. God, how long I've dreamt of this, he thought.

He leaned forward and took one of the now protruding nipples into his mouth and sucked on it softly, then moved onto the other one, taking turns to kiss, suck and roll his tongue around each of them. Sandra held him in her arms tightly, caressed him gently and whispered sweet nothings to him.

Jack could feel his wife's heart pounding faster and faster.

He sat up and laid her back onto the bed, then slipped his thumbs into the sides of her knickers and peeled them off her body in one fell swoop. She looked embarrassed. 'Can we get under the quilt, Jack?' she begged,

'What's the matter, honey?' said Jack.

'It's been a long time for me too, darling,' she whispered.

Jack pulled back the quilt and she quickly slipped into the bed; she pulled the quilt up to the top of her nose so that just her eyes protruded – she looked like a frightened child.

Jack slipped into bed next to her and put his arms around her; they cuddled together for a long time.

Jack then stroked her legs and caressed her thighs, slowly moving around to her inner thighs, feeling her wince like a virgin bride on her wedding night. He stroked both her inner thighs softly and he felt her shiver. He was hoping to turn her on to the pleasures that they had both enjoyed so much before his arrest but he could see that she had acquired a shyness only found in someone left untouched for many years. He moved gently, trying to gain her confidence which in turn would help her to relax. He moved his hand higher and she stiffened, her body tense in anticipation.

'Relax, honey,' Jack said, and she loosened a little. Jack went straight to her pussy and stroked her gently, making a conscious effort not to be too rough with her. He slid his finger along the line of her softness and her legs parted; Jack could feel the wetness of her body and he inserted a finger into her soft warm flesh, not deeply at first but gradually penetrating deeper and deeper until he could go no further.

He played for a while, touching and tormenting her, listening to the changes in her breathing pattern and the little moans that she let slip while squirming around the bed. Her body now meeting his finger in short rhythmic thrusts, he felt that she was as ready as she ever would be. He rolled his body over on top of hers, his already erect prick throbbing in anticipation as he lay between her thighs. He entered her soft warm body and began to move rhythmically, first softly, gently, then gaining momentum, then slowly again until he felt that he could hold back no longer.

Four years of pent-up emotion released into his lovely, sexy wife. They lay there joined together for some time laughing and joking about their amateurish attempt at lovemaking.

Jack said, 'It was like trying to get a telegraph pole through the eye of a needle.'

'I know,' she said laughing, 'I'll probably not walk for a week.'

'And I was hoping that you'd carry me downstairs,' laughed Jack. 'My legs have gone weak.'

'Good God! Look at the time,' she said. 'We'll be late for the ferry.'

They rushed to get dressed and went downstairs, Jack first and Sandra behind him sheepishly, wondering if any of the people downstairs had known what they were up to – after all they had only gone up to collect Sandra's bags and that was over an hour ago. Too late for worrying now, she thought, and anyway they were finally going home.

Jack had a bad time on the ferry on the way back across to the mainland. He had a panic attack as he wasn't used to all the noise and people moving around so fast – after all, everyday life in prison had been so slow and mundane.

Once Jack left the ferry the problem disappeared as quickly as it had arisen, and he drove home without further interruption.

It was only a four-day leave and then it was back to reality; it had been a good leave for Jack but there was still much hard work to be done before his release.

Jack still hadn't recovered from the parole refusal that he had got earlier in the year; he was still gutted by it and so was his wife, but now that he had returned on time from his home leave and also because he was now a Cat 'C' prisoner, Jack started to look at other options and one of those options was to move to a Cat 'C' prison which was closer to his home and which would save his wife a six-hundred-mile round trip to visit him on the island each month.

It took several more months before his application was sorted out and he was transferred to Risley prison in Cheshire, which was only a few miles from his home. However, only a few weeks later he was offered a move from Risley to a Cat 'D' prison seventy miles away. Jack was told that Sudbury prison in Derbyshire had a system called compacts which meant that every prisoner went home for the weekend each month. Jack jumped at the offer and was promptly moved to open conditions where he remained for two more years until his release.

Chapter Two

A Taste of Freedom

Jack had waited a long, long time for this moment. Freedom at last as he walked away from the prison towards the waiting car; his wife and children had practically camped outside for half the night in anticipation of his release.

After all these years, the nightmare was finally over.

Sandra got out of the car as he approached; she went to the rear of the car and opened the boot to accommodate the bags of clothes and the junk that Jack had accumulated over the years. Jack threw the bags into the boot and Sandra closed it. They put their arms around each other and kissed.

'We'll soon be home,' whispered Sandra.

'Let's go, then,' said Jack.

Jack got into the driver's seat and his daughters, who were sitting in the back of the car, put their arms around his neck and kissed him.

'Time to go,' said Jack.

'Fasten your seat belts, girls, we're flying home,' he laughed and they laughed with him.

It took one hour and forty-five minutes for them to get home but Jack was no longer in a rush; a great burden had been lifted off him that day and he was at a new peace with himself. He was content with his lot for now.

Jack turned into his driveway and there to his amazement was a giant yellow ribbon tied around a dilapidated willow tree.

Jack smiled and turned to his wife who was also smiling.

'Sorry about the tree,' she said. 'It would have taken too long to grow an oak.'

They all laughed.

Jack was impressed with her thoughtfulness.

They all left the car and walked to the front door. Sandra unlocked the door and as they went inside, she turned to Jack and said, 'Welcome home, honey.'

'Thanks, babe, it's good to be home and even better is the fact that this time I don't have to go back,' said Jack.

Not now, not ever, he thought as they walked through the house to the kitchen.

'I'm tired,' Jack said. 'I could do with an hour's sleep,' he hinted to his wife. She knew what he meant and smiled at him. 'First things first,' she said. 'I'll put the kettle on – we've been outside that jail for hours.'

'I hope it was worth it,' said Jack jokingly.

'It will be,' she laughed, 'it definitely will be.'

The four of them chatted incessantly around the kitchen table as they sipped their tea, the girls finishing theirs first and slipping outside to play.

'We'll be back later!' they shouted as the back door slammed behind them with a bit of help from the wind.

'They're growing up fast,' Jack said.

'Aren't they just,' mused his wife.

'Anyway, come to think of it, it's got its benefits too, you know,' Jack said laughing.

'And what might they be?' she giggled.

'Great minds think alike!' he said as he took her by the hand and they ran upstairs, laughing and giggling like naughty schoolkids.

They resurfaced a couple of hours later just in time to organise a meal for their now hungry daughters.

'Playing doesn't half make you hungry, Mum,' one of them complained.

Doesn't it just! thought the now ravenous Jack. He looked at his wife and caught her eye. 'Hungry too, dear?' she grinned.

'Playing doesn't half make you hungry, Mum,' he jested and they both burst into laughter. The children looked at them oddly.

'I don't see what's so funny,' said one of them.

'You will one day,' said Mum almost without thinking and not really aiming her reply at anyone in particular.

After a few weeks at home Jack took his family to Florida for a six-week holiday; they were still trying to get to know each other properly and the girls were still getting used to having a male around the house. The positioning of the toilet seat was the constant source of endless debate, as was facial hair in the bathroom sink, all of which was new to Jack's daughters, who had become accustomed to their all-female environment.

Their main visitors to the house over the years and the only people to have stayed overnight were their grandmother and their aunt.

Jack could understand their hostility to his intrusion; his untidiness in general and his maleness was not easy for any of them to get used to.

He hoped that a few weeks' holiday in Florida and the fact that they would all be in unfamiliar surroundings would bring them closer together. As it was now, Jack was the stranger in his own house and he found it difficult to come to terms with that.

The girls had always wanted to go to Disneyland in America and Jack had always promised that he would take them there, so it was two weeks in Orlando first of all and then over to Bradenton in Tampa to stay with friends for four weeks over Christmas and the new year.

It had been a great holiday and they had all enjoyed themselves immensely, but it had also been tiring, especially for Jack who had not been used to so much activity for years.

He felt that his age was catching up with him. He had celebrated his forty-second birthday while in Florida but at this moment in time he felt much older; the holiday had drained him and the Florida sunshine had burnt him mercilessly – he was almost glad to be back home.

There had been many messages for Jack on his return; the answerphone had run out of space and there were numerous notes that had been pushed through his door. Many other callers had rung Jack's brother Charles when they had tried and failed to contact Jack. Charles passed on many messages and he was useful at times, but he lived in a different world to Jack's.

Charles had a wife and three children, and he had a nine-to-five regular job that would have killed Jack. Jack was not a man who liked routine; he never was and now after his spell in prison he hated it even more.

Jack liked to be his own man; he didn't mind work but felt that he had to be in charge of his own destiny. He liked working for himself – that way he could decide what to do and who to do it for, and more to the point, how much he would be paid for his skills. There were not many offers of work like that in the local job centre but in truth Jack was not even looking. He had a plan and now that some of his old friends and some recent acquaintances were beginning to get in touch with him, Jack could see that his plan was now more than a possibility.

Later when the girls were in bed, Jack and Sandra were sat on the sofa huddled together watching TV when Sandra said, 'What's going to happen now, Jack?'

'About what, honey?'

'About what you're going to do for a living.'

'I'm not sure.'

'I think that you've already made your mind up, all these messages on the answerphone off all these strange people – you're up to something and you're going to finish up back in jail.'

'What do you want me to do, honey?' asked Jack for the first time.

'I want you to get a proper job. I want you to be here permanently with me and the girls, not just part time in between prison sentences. I know that you were stitched up by the police and the customs and that you've lost everything that you'd worked hard for all your life, but you've still got me and the girls, we can start again, we've started from scratch before and built a successful business. I've got faith in you, honey, you can do it again, we can do it together.'

'Do you really think that I can do it again at my age without having to resort to skulduggery?'

'Honey, you can do anything. What's happened to all the dreams that you had? All the hopes for the future? Don't give up on your dreams, hon', a man without a dream has got nothing. You've always had a dream to follow and in the past you've made some of them come true, you can do it again. Let's not resort to risking you going back to prison – once in anyone's lifetime is enough, believe me once is one time too many.'

'What should we do first then, babe? Look for a small business that's for sale?'

'No, what I want you to do first is destroy all those phone numbers and addresses that you've been collecting all these years. Let's cut off all the dead wood and start afresh, let's do it now, let's make a clean break from the past and go for it, that's what I want, Jack. I don't want the police kicking the door in every ten minutes, I don't want to sit up all night worrying that you've been arrested when you're late home.'

Jack thought about it for a while; it was a serious possibility but it also had a serious downside – what if he ever needed any of the numbers again in the future? While Jack sat there thinking, Sandra got the book of numbers out of the cupboard, along with a box which was full of little bits of paper with numbers, names and addresses. She waved them under Jack's nose. 'It's now or never, hon',' she said.

'You'll have to rip them up yourself, babe, it's too heartbreaking for me to do.'

Sandra sat there in front of Jack until she had ripped every single piece of paper into shreds – the numbers and addresses were all gone for ever.

Jack was now without serious contact into the world of villainy.

Jack felt a sense of loss like he'd lost a friend.

'Feel better now, Jack?' Sandra asked.

'No.'

'Well I do,' she whispered as she snuggled back up to him on the sofa.

The following weekend Jack and Sandra scoured their local paper, looking for small businesses for sale but there was nothing suitable that Jack fancied. They looked through other magazines and the *Daltons Weekly*; although there were some ideas that Jack took a liking to, they were much too far afield for him to bother with. 'I'm fed up, San,' Jack shouted.

'Don't give up, honey, we'll find something, we'll build a dream somewhere.'

'I hope that it's soon, hon', because the money that we've got won't last for ever.' After some weeks of looking, Jack found for sale a skip hire business that he was interested in; there were five trucks and fifty skips plus a large yard and some office buildings. Jack was happy at the price that it was offered at, as long as the property stood up to the agent's valuation, and the company's books were in order. He could see no problem raising the finances to buy this business.

Two weeks later with the value of the property agreed and the accounts audited, Jack set off for his appointment with his bank manager. It was not good news. The bank refused the loan which Jack desperately needed on the grounds that the property and business that he wanted to buy was out of Jack's credit range with the small amount of cash that he had plus his house as collateral.

Jack was told that he either needed more of his own cash or more collateral to the tune of a hundred thousand pounds if the bank was going to consider the loan.

Jack was dismayed; he'd shown the bank manager that he could meet the payments of the loan with the money from the business as it stood now. It was obvious from the books that there was enough money coming in from the council contract alone to cover the loan payments.

The bank manager was adamant. 'No additional collateral, no loan,' he'd said. Jack went home to discuss it with Sandra.

'Maybe we could borrow some money off my dad,' she said.

'Over my dead body,' Jack replied.

'Well it was just an idea, honey.'

'I know babe, I didn't mean to snap at you, but it's been a long day.'

The next day Jack went to see his mother, who agreed to put her house up as collateral for the business after Jack had persuaded her that it could not fail, and that it was already making money with a steady contract from the local council.

But even with his mother's house for collateral, Jack still had a twenty thousand pounds shortfall if he was to obtain a loan from the bank.

Jack went home to contemplate his next move.

Sandra rang her mother and explained how hard Jack was trying to make a straight living and the difficulties he was having raising the collateral. After a long chat, Sandra persuaded her mother to put her house up to cover the twenty thousand pounds shortfall that Jack was having trouble raising.

Within a month Jack moved into his new premises and took over the business. The previous occupant had stripped it bare, even taking all the light bulbs with him. Jack thought Sam Edwards was a very strange man.

He checked over the trucks that he had just bought and considered them all to be death traps. Jack and the fitter that he had employed worked day and night to make them roadworthy.

It was two weeks later before Jack got around to checking any paperwork and when he did, he was not a happy man.

'There's definitely something wrong, Sandra.'

'What's wrong, Jack?'

'I don't know... I wish that I did.'

The next day Jack checked all the tachographs in his wagons to see if he'd been the subject of any fraud by the drivers.

'No, Sandra it's not a scam – it's the work, it's just not coming in. The council contract is still being carried out and we'll get paid off that at the end of the month, but that alone will only just keep our heads above water – other than that we'll have to find some more work.'

'Maybe you should put some ads in the local papers and drop a few business cards off at local businesses.'

'Yeah, that might be worth a try.'

Jack tried all ways possible to make the business generate more money but to no avail; it was only the council contract that the company had held for nearly five years that kept the repayments going on the bank loan.

Jack worked night and day to keep the business running; it wasn't unusual for Sandra to drive down to the workshop late at night with sandwiches, and a flask of tea to make sure that he was at least eating and drinking something.

Two weeks later Jack had to lay off two of the drivers; there was not enough work coming in to justify their wages, and it didn't look like it was going to get any better for a while.

Jack had only been trading for five months when a letter arrived at his office from the local council telling him that the contract that his company held with them on a yearly basis would not be renewed as from two months from the date of the letter. Jack nearly collapsed as he knew that the council contract was the only thing between him and the bankruptcy courts,

Jack stormed down to the council offices and demanded to see whoever was in charge of the department concerned. A few minutes later a young man in his mid-twenties appeared. 'Can I help you, sir?' he said politely.

'Damn right you can,' Jack said showing him the letter. 'What's all this about?'

'Yes I see,' said the council worker. 'What seems to be the problem?'

'What seems to be the problem?' repeated Jack almost screaming. 'I'll tell you what the problem is – I've bought a business which looked a good bet on paper, only to see it almost collapse in a matter of a few months, and then this letter appeared this morning to put the final nail in the coffin, because without that contract my business is dead.'

'I'm sorry, sir.'

'You're bleedin' sorry, how do you think that I feel? My house, my mother's house, and my mother-in-law's house are all tied to this business. If I lose the business then we will all lose our homes.'

'What can I do about it?'

'You can give me the contract back for a start.'

'I can't do that, sir, it's been out to tender.'

'Why haven't I been given an option to tender for it?'

'I don't know, sir. I just know that someone else has got the job, starting in two months.'

Jack could tell by looking at this guy that there was more to this than he was saying, but here was not the place to find out more. He left without saying another word.

Later that day the council worker left the building to go home and Jack followed him to the multi-storey car park where his car was parked. As he reached his car, he realised that there was someone behind him. Startled, he turned around quickly and saw Jack standing there. He remembered Jack's face from that morning's exchange of words. 'What do you want?' he gasped.

'I want to know the truth about that contract.'

'I told you this morning.'

'What you told me this morning is bullshit.'

'I don't know what you mean.'

'Well you'd better learn quick or we're going to get physical, and it's a long drop off this car park.'

'Whoa, hang on a minute, I can see that you're angry and a bit unstable, just calm yourself down a little.'

'If you don't tell me the truth, I'll show you just how unstable I am, and I'll plead insanity in court.'

This last statement really shook up the man from the council; he had visions of his blood and guts splattered on the pavement below passing through his mind, and he didn't care too much for the idea. 'Listen, I'll tell you, but you never got it from me, okay?'

'That sounds fair to me,' said Jack.

'A copper, an Inspector Graylor, came into our office and spoke to my bosses; he told them that you were an ex-convict and that you were a bad lot, and he recommended that they should cancel any contracts that your company may have with us. It was a coincidence that the contract was due for renewal at the end of next month; if that copper hadn't come into our office then the contract would have been renewed as a matter of course as it always has been before. I'm sorry, mate, I'm just doing my job.'

'Police pressure, eh!' Jack said sadly as he stared at the council worker for a while, then he turned and walked away, much to the relief of the latter. Jack thought about Inspector Graylor as he drove home; it was a name not unfamiliar to Jack. Inspector Graylor had been one of the coppers who had fabricated evidence against Jack which had culminated in Jack going to prison for eleven years. After Jack's arrest, and when not in the presence of any of his fellow officers, Graylor had returned to Jack's house on numerous occasions, using the flimsiest of excuses, and then always getting around to the subject of Sandra being left on her own with the children.

'I might be able to help you,' he'd said, always followed by some sexual connotations. Sandra always refused his help, and his advances. The last time that he called was just before Jack was sentenced, and he'd said to Sandra that Jack was going away for a long time, and that she was going to have a lot of cold and lonely nights. He then left his phone number, telling her to ring him when she got lonely. She never did.

Sandra had kept Jack informed of all this bent copper's actions, and Jack said he'd keep it all in mind for future reference.

Jack went home and told Sandra about losing the council contract. Sandra burst into tears.

'What are we going to do, Jack?'

'I don't know, honey.'

'We'll lose everything, Jack, and so will our mothers.'

'Not if I can help it,' said Jack hopefully. Only the thought of helping Sandra and their mothers out of this mess that he'd got them into gave him the determination to carry on fighting, though at that moment in time he knew not how.

Jack was now at an all-time low.

As the next few days went by things only got worse – the bills continued to come in, but there was no money coming in to cover them, only the last of the council money which was to keep the bank at bay for a few more weeks.

Jack laid off the rest of his employees and tried to run the business on his own, with him doing any driving that came up and Sandra answering the phones.

Jack and Sandra were at the office when an old friend who they hadn't seen for many years arrived, looking for Sam Edwards, the previous owner.

'Hello, Nick, how ya doing?' said Jack.

'I'm okay, Jack, where's Sam?'

'He's not here any longer, I bought the place off him.'

'*You* Jack? You bought the place off Slippery Sam?'

'Slippery Sam?' Jack and Sandra said in unison.

'Yeah, Slippery Sam, he was one of the biggest drug dealers in the area,' said Nick.

'And he was putting the money through a dead company, and making it look like a profitable enterprise?' said the stunned Jack.

'You've got it, Jack.'

'He must have seen me coming.'

'He mustn't have known it was you, Jack,' said the knowing Nick.

'Maybe not, but he will one day, if I ever get out of this mess.'

Jack locked the premises up and went home with Sandra.

'What are we going to do, Jack?'

'I'm thinking, honey, I'm thinking hard, I wish that I still had those phone numbers.'

'I don't, Jack.'

'What do you want us to do? Live in a fucking cardboard box?' Jack screamed.

Sandra burst into tears. 'What's happening to us, Jack? After all we've been through!'

'These things are sent to try us, honey, we've tried it your way, now I've got to try it mine.'

A couple of days later one of Jack's daughters came in from school and said, 'Can I have a computer, Dad?'

'Not at the moment, darling, but as soon as I can afford one, you can have whichever one you like,' Jack said rather optimistically.

Later that night Jack was laying in bed with Sandra when he suddenly jumped up shouting, 'That's it, that's it.'

'That's what, honey?' Sandra said while trying to recover her breath after Jack had frightened her half to death with his screaming. 'All those names and addresses that you ripped up, I've got them on a floppy disk somewhere in the attic, amongst all that junk that I brought home from the nick.'

'Be careful, Jack, please be careful.'

'What choice have I got, honey? Tell me what choice have I got?'

The next day Jack took the boxes from the attic and searched until he found what he was looking for – a box of floppy disks. He borrowed a computer from Steve Donoghue, a friend of Jack's who was in the computer business.

Jack went through all the disks one at a time until he found the one that had the list of names and addresses hidden on it. Jack picked out a few numbers that he thought would be useful, then he went to a telephone box half a mile from his house and dialled.

Jack made arrangements to meet some of his old contacts.

Jack met up with most of his contacts away from his house as he did not wish to be seen with anyone who might later become a liability if he could be connected to them. Jack also met them personally to avoid speaking on the telephone. For business matters, Jack also avoided using his own telephone like the plague. Using a home telephone had been the downfall of many a good but lazy or foolish man.

Big Brother was out there watching and listening, thought Jack. For safety's sake we must assume that we are under surveillance, so as not to become complacent. There is no need to become paranoid, thought Jack, just careful, just bloody careful.

One of the messages on Jack's answerphone was from a guy called Tooting Tony from London. He was a major cannabis distributor for several of the large importers; he wanted a meeting with Jack and it sounded pretty urgent.

Jack drove to a public call box and rang him to arrange a meeting; it was decided that they would meet in the Paradise Lost nightclub in Watford the following Saturday. It had been quite some time since Jack had entered a nightclub, since he no longer owned one of his own, and he had long since given up the precarious occupation of being a bouncer. He found that he no longer had a reason nor the inclination to frequent such establishments.

He did, however, harbour the wish that he would like to own another nightclub one day.

'It's been a long time, Toot,' said Jack.

'Could be worse,' said Toot, 'we could still be in the big house.'

'Fuck that for a game of marbles,' said Jack. 'I'd have been nutted off by now, I'm surprised that I lasted this long.'

They both laughed at the thought.

'Let's find somewhere to talk, Jack,' said Toot, while ogling some waitress in a skimpy dress. 'Just something she threw on.'

'Yes, and she nearly fuckin' missed!' laughed Jack.

They moved to the restaurant in the club and found a quiet corner.

'What's the crack, then, Toot? What's going down?' Jack enquired.

'Well, it's like this, Jack, I've been moving five hundred kees a week for one of the big firms down here and it's been no problem until now. I've used the same five buyers every week and each have taken a hundred kees and distributed it in their own area.'

'Get to the point, Toot, or we'll be here all night,' Jack demanded.

'The point is that one of my buyers has been busted and I'd laid the gear on to him – he would have paid me tomorrow. But getting back to the point, I hadn't told this firm that I was working for that I'd laid the gear on to this guy.'

'Holy shit!' said Jack. 'That was not one of your better decisions.'

'You can say that again,' Toot mumbled.

'What are you going to do about it then, Toot, how are you going to cover it?' Jack quizzed.

'Well, Jack, I was hoping that you'd help me out,' Toot pleaded.

'I've not got that sort of money, not these days, well, not yet,' said Jack.

'I understand that you haven't got the money, but maybe you could have a word with this firm. They'll listen to you,

Jack. All I need is a bit of time, a few weeks and I'll cover it,' Toot said, more in the manner of a begging letter.

'And why will they listen to me, Toot?' said Jack.

'It's the 'A' team,' said Toot.

'Fucking hell!' Jack shouted, causing other people in the restaurant to turn and look at where the sharp outburst had come from.

'Listen, Toot, these people are friends of mine but we've never done this sort of business before. I'll have to think about it.'

They ordered a meal and sat there reminiscing for a while as they ate it.

'I'll order some wine,' said Toot.

'Just a coffee for me,' said Jack. 'It's gonna be a long night'.

Later, Toot wanted Jack to go back to his house, but Jack insisted on going back to the hotel that he'd booked earlier. He needed time to think about what his next move would be. They arranged to meet the next afternoon at two o'clock in McDonalds.

Jack arrived early and Toot was already there. Jack eyed up the other people in the place, looking for anything that might signal a set-up. Jack was not the most trusting of guys these days – experience had taught him well. They sat in a corner away from any other customers with just a coffee each on the table in front of them.

'Here's the deal then,' said Jack. 'I'll talk to the 'A' team and if they go for it, I want the spare hundred kees a week that you've got and I want it at the right price. I don't want anyone else to know about our arrangement, not even the 'A' team. I'll let you know how I want it done later.'

'Sounds fair to me, Jack,' said Toot with a sigh of relief.

'We'll see what develops when I've spoken to the 'A' team then,' said Jack as he got up to leave. 'I'm going home and it's a long drive. I'll ring you later tonight.'

Jack turned and left but he didn't go straight home; he went to see the 'A' team. He explained Toot's predicament and they were angry as they had told Toot only to do cash deals unless they told him otherwise; they were really miffed and wanted to kill him. After a while they calmed down and listened to reason; it was a way that they would get their money back and keep the trade running through Toot, who, although he was a bit stupid at times, always shifted the gear and in big lumps, too.

Jack drove home; it had been a long couple of days and he was shattered.

'Wake me up at ten, honey,' he said to his wife as he walked through the door and straight up the stairs to bed.

'Ten in the morning?' she answered.

'Wishful thinking,' said Jack, 'but unfortunately I've got to ring someone at ten o'clock tonight.'

Sandra woke Jack at ten and brought him a cup of tea.

'Thanks, honey,' he said as he sipped the tea, hoping to glean some energy from it.

'Should I run you a bath, hon'?' she asked.

'I'll have one when I get back in about fifteen minutes,' replied Jack. 'I've got to dash down the road to a public phone box. Have you got any change?' he inquired as he rapidly got dressed and ran down the stairs.

'There's some on the kitchen table,' Sandra answered.

Jack grabbed it on his way through as he disappeared out of the door and into the night.

The phone rang for ages, then just as Jack was about to put it down Toot answered.

'Where the fuck were you?' Jack quizzed.

'I was on the bleeding toilet, mate, honest,' he pleaded.

'Okay, okay, right then,' said Jack. 'This is the position – the 'A' team have gone for it.' There was a scream of joy down the phone that almost deafened Jack.

'Thanks mate, I owe you one,' said Toot.

'I know you do, Toot, and I'll be collecting,' stated Jack in a meaningful tone. 'I'll ring you again in a couple of days to let you know about the first delivery.'

'No problem, no problem at all, Jack.'

'Let's hope not,' said Jack. 'By the way, have you got the stuff already?'

'Sure thing, pal, sure thing,' Toot repeated.

Jack said, 'I'll be in touch,' and with that he put the phone down and went home to have a long soak in the bath with his wife. Jack loved these tender moments that he shared with Sandra and after being away from her for so many years, he treasured every minute of her company.

The next day Jack was up and out of the house early; there was much to be done and not a lot of time in which to do it. He found a telephone box and dialled a number from his pocket diary.

'Hello,' came a voice from the other end of the line.

'Hello, Big Dave,' said Jack, recognising Dave's thunderous tones.

Dave's tone softened. 'Hello, Jack, it's been a long time, old friend.'

'Hasn't it just, mate, hasn't it just?' Jack said, repeating himself. 'Are you still open for business, Dave?'

'You'd better believe it, matey, one has to earn a crust, you know,' Dave laughed. 'Are you free this afternoon? 'Cos if you are then I'll be up to see you. I've got a deal that you will definitely be interested in.'

'If it's one of yours, Jack, then I probably will be. You'll never change will you, Jack, eh? Jack Dunkerley, the man with a plan.'

They both laughed.

'I'll be in this afternoon, Jack, anytime you like I'm here all day.'

'Catch ya later, then,' said Jack.

'Yeah, later,' Dave replied as he put down the receiver.

Jack arrived at Big Dave's house around midday; he was welcomed by Big Dave with the sort of hug that would have turned cars into little blocks of metal.

'Welcome home, Jack,' Dave shouted down Jack's ear.

'Thanks,' Jack gasped almost breathless, 'you've got a grip like a bleeding vice.'

'That's what comes of carrying all those big bags of gear about, mate,' roared Dave with a belly laugh that would have drowned out the engines of Concorde. They sat down to a cup of tea brought in by Dave's wife who was a tiny elfish little thing – the complete opposite of Dave who was a giant of a man even compared to Jack who was no midget at six foot three and weighing in at a good sixteen stone. Dave's wife put down the tea and left the room; she mumbled that she had things to do. Jack thanked her for the tea but she never looked back as she left the room, closing the door behind her.

Jack supposed that she had got used to Big Dave's wheeling and dealing over the years and this was her way of dealing with it.

'Right then, Dave, let's get down to business – how much puff can you shift per week?' asked Jack.

'Depends what it is and how much it is,' said Dave.

'It's soap bar and the price will be right,' said Jack. 'Someone owes me a favour, a big favour, and I'm collecting, so how much can you move?'

'Twenty, maybe twenty-five a week,' Dave replied.

'Is that all Dave? asked Jack. 'You were moving that much years ago.'

'And that's why I'm not in jail, Jack. I stick to the same buyers that I've been with for years. There's too many grasses about these days, too many people wanting to know other people's business when it's got fuck all to do with them; they should keep their fucking noses out,' Dave said angrily. 'Too many good guys doing serious porridge, just for talking too much to the wrong guy, best sticking to the old guys that have been around a long time. They're tried and tested, Jack, it's too dangerous to get involved with newcomers; these undercover pigs are all over the place nowadays, you've got to be careful, so bloody careful.'

'I know,' said Jack, 'but sometimes you've got to take risks, you've just got to minimise them.'

'Not me, mate,' said Dave. 'I've stuck to this game plan for nigh on fifteen years and I'm staying with it. I might never be a millionaire but it's a good earner and it beats working for a living.'

He was laughing but he was serious and he meant every word. Dave had no intention of going to prison if it could be avoided.

'This is what I want you to do,' Jack said. 'I want you to buy a car from the auction, just a banger with a couple of months' tax on it, use a false name and address, get a spare key cut, and when the time is right I'll let you know where to park the car, a pub car park or the like. Leave the spare key on the driver's side rear wheel, so it's out of sight from any would-be joyriders. I'll ring you the next day and let you know where to pick the car up from. The gear will be bolted in under the rear seat, so all you have to do is get the car collected, take it to your lock-up, get the gear out and sell it.'

'What if the gear is a load of crap?' Dave said, then wishing he hadn't opened his mouth. The look he got from Jack could have killed at fifty paces.

'Sorry Jack,' he said and meant it; there would never be a problem with anything from Jack. His reputation was renowned and if there ever was any unforeseen eventuality then Jack was prepared to stand the loss himself. That's how confident he was in his own capabilities.

'Should I count you in for twenty-five kee a week, Dave?'

'It's pushing it a bit, but I should manage to handle it,' Dave said hopefully.

'Right then,' said Jack, 'I'll be in touch soon, sort the motor out as soon as poss.'

'It's done,' said Dave nonchalantly.

'Catch ya later, then,' said Jack.

'*Adios amigo*,' Dave replied in his best spaghetti western Mexican accent.

Jack got into his wife's car and headed for home, his brain ticking away at a rate of knots that would have blown a gasket if he'd been an engine. He racked his brains thinking of who he could next approach to take some of the hundred kees that he had coming soon; it had to be someone in a different area, too, as it would be no use putting it all out in the same place. First of all it would flood the market and take longer to sell and, secondly, it would cause the price to drop, and that was the last thing that Jack wanted to do.

Suddenly Jack had a brainwave – a name and a face appeared like a vision.

'Got it!' Jack mumbled to himself. 'Rage! I've not seen him for years.'

Rage was a cross between a Hell's Angel and a leftover from a phase one hippie, though where he had acquired the name 'Rage' from God only knows – he was one of the quietest men that Jack had ever met, or maybe that was because he was always stoned.

Such is life, thought Jack, such is life.

Jack turned the car around and headed for Rage's house. When he arrived at the house he was met by Rage's wife. 'Maybe she's called Mrs Rage,' Jack chuckled to himself.

'Is Rage about, love?' Jack enquired.

'I saw him last week,' she replied.

'Last week?' Jack said questioningly.

'Yeah last week,' she repeated. 'He doesn't live here any more; he got his own place a couple of years ago and we parted company. He comes around now and again to see the kids.'

'Where does he live nowadays?' Jack asked.

'Only a few miles up the road. If you hang on a minute I'll get you the address and phone number,' she offered.

Jack waited for her to return with the information, then with the details in his hand he left and headed for Rage's new abode. It didn't take him long to find the house. Jack parked the car some distance away and walked up to the house.

Jack knocked on the door; there was no reply at first but Jack noticed some movement of the net curtains and so he waited patiently. A couple of minutes later the figure of Rage appeared in the doorway, an older, more weather-beaten face than the one Jack had remembered. Probably due to years of drug abuse, thought Jack, as he followed the figure into the house.

'Where've you been, man?' said Rage in that old hippie-like tone that was ever familiar to Jack even after all these years.

'I've been in the jailhouse, that's where I've been,' Jack retorted.

'Yeah, I remember hearing about the case, man, it was a fit-up, wasn't it?' asked Rage.

'It was more than a fit-up, mate, it was a fucking catastrophe for me, my wife, my kids, and my business. They fucked my life up,' said Jack in anger.

'Yeah, I knew it wasn't you, Jack,' said Rage knowingly.

'And how did you know that then, Rage?' asked Jack.

'Class 'A', man, class 'A', not your scene, man, not your scene. I mean let's have it right, Jack, you're no angel by a long shot but you're not a class 'A' merchant, you're not a dealer in death, are you? Well not the drug sort anyway,'

Rage added after a quick rethink and remembering some of the fracas that Jack had been involved in, where the offending body had been left bloodstained and motionless as Jack made a quick exit.

'You're right, Rage, you're dead fucking right,' said Jack, drifting into deep thought of how the customs and the police had conspired together to put him in prison and seize all his assets, assets that had taken him a lifetime to acquire. Never again would he leave himself open to having his assets seized. He had studied long and hard while in prison; he'd read all the Scope International books and more. There wasn't much that Jack didn't know about off shore bank accounts, numbered accounts, and the *anstalts* of Austria and Liechtenstein; this time, legal or otherwise, there would be no trace of his money.

'Jack!' shouted Rage.

'What's the matter?' asked a startled Jack.

'I was talking to myself, man, that's what the fuck was up. You were miles away. You've been in jail too long, banged up in a cell with only your own company, it can do strange things to you, man.'

'Maybe you've got a point there, Rage, my mate, maybe I need some therapy,' Jack said laughing. Rage joined in the laughter.

'What you need, Jack, is a fucking big spliff with some serious ganja in it,' said Rage. They both fell about laughing.

'Not for me, Rage, but I do take the point, maybe I do need to relax a bit more, maybe in a year or two when business is finished with. Maybe then I'll get away with the missus for a while and take it easy, maybe even retire. I've got plenty to attend to first.'

'Unfinished business to attend to as well, eh, Jack?'

'Something like that,' Jack said as his mind wandered to thoughts of the Indian guy who had set him up and almost destroyed his life; the thought of this guy made Jack angry. I've waited this long, thought Jack. I can wait a bit longer.

'Mind wandering again?' inquired Rage.

'Just a little,' laughed Jack, 'but nothing to worry about, eh?'

'You need time to adjust, man, you need to absorb the realities of the big bad world, then you'll settle back into the swing of things without drifting off into dreamland every ten minutes,' said Rage wisely.

'It's not that bad,' said Jack. 'It's just that you've touched on a few nerve endings, which made me digress a little. Anyway, let's talk business – how many kees can you move in a week?'

'Normally if it's good gear then I can do fifty a week no trouble but at the moment there's nothing about, it's dry around here. I've had customers screaming at me for weeks.'

'Your troubles are over,' said Jack. 'From now on you will get your gear from me; it will be regular and it will always be pukka, the best. Any problems and there's a money back guarantee. This is how it works...'

Jack went on to explain to Rage about buying a car from the auction and where to leave it and where to hide the key, the same as he had explained earlier to Big Dave.

Jack had stayed at Rage's house much longer than he had wanted to – the time flew by while they were discussing business and old times. Jack liked Rage in a funny kind of way. He liked his odd mannerisms, his hippie-like lifestyle; it was like he was stuck in a time warp from the sixties and the world could change as much as it liked but he wasn't altering one iota.

Jack left Rage's house, got into his wife's car and headed home. Jack had promised Sandra that he'd be back for about four and it was now gone six o'clock. He was sure that she'd understand; she knew that he was doing something but she didn't know what it was and she didn't want to know – Sandra was happier not knowing. If she had known what Jack was plotting then she would only have worried about him, and Jack thought that she had worried enough over the years when he had not been there to support her.

He didn't want her to worry about him again, ever.

Jack walked into the house and straight into the kitchen. 'I'm starving,' he said to Sandra.

'Your dinner's in the dog,' she joked.

'Warm the dog up, I'll eat the dog,' Jack responded. They both laughed in unison.

'You're late for tea again, honey,' she said.

'It's getting to be a habit, isn't it, love?' said Jack with a sad look on his face that was begging for attention.

Sandra stepped forward and kissed Jack's forehead. 'There, there,' she said in her best mother-to-sad-child voice. Jack looked up at her and saw only love in her eyes; she was pleased to see him whatever the time may be.

Jack got up and kissed her passionately; she responded the same. After a minute or two they separated. 'I'll put your tea out, Jack,' she said.

'I'll just have a quick wash,' said Jack. 'I'll be back in a minute.'

Jack came back and started to eat his tea. 'Where are the girls?' he inquired.

'They wanted to stay at my mother's, so I've left them both there,' she said with a huge mischievous smile spreading across her face.

'Sounds like a cue for an early night,' Jack grinned.

'We've got all night – there's no rush,' said Sandra.

'There might not be a rush for you, honeypot, but for me I'm ready now,' said Jack dreamily while thinking what he would be getting for dessert.

'Finish your tea, Jack,' she implored.

Sandra disappeared upstairs while Jack finished his tea. She returned a few minutes later, but now her previously ponytailed hair was loose about her head, and she was wearing a low-cut top showing off her large cleavage. She was also wearing the shortest miniskirt that Jack had ever seen, which showed off the top of her black stockings and a portion of white flesh at the top of her leg which contrasted with her dark clothing and made her look like the sexiest woman in the world. And to Jack she was.

'Wanna see what's for afters?' she offered in her sexiest voice.

'Don't mind if I do,' said Jack, who now had an erection that was throbbing to get out and was having its blood supply cut off by his ever-tightening jeans.

Sandra took his hand and led him into their lounge. She sat him down in the armchair and released his now bulging prick from its denim cage; she massaged him gently, taking his throbbing shaft into her hand and tormented him by pulling back on his foreskin while teasing the end of his now glowing shaft with her tongue. She licked him and then moved her head away sharply, making him wince. His legs stiffened in anticipation then relaxed again; this happened many times as she teased him, massaging his balls at the same time. He began to breathe heavily. He moved forward in the chair; she pushed him back down again. Still tormenting his erect shaft, she moved her head down to lick his throbbing prick once more, but this time she took his prick into her mouth and moved her head up and down like a piston. Her eyes watched him squirm with pleasure while she enjoyed tormenting him this way. His balls were filling up at a rapid rate and he could hold back no longer; he pushed her back to the floor and crawled on top of her; she wrapped her legs around him. He loved the way that she had dressed to turn him on and she had succeeded one hundred per cent. He felt the flesh at the top of her stockinged leg – it was soft and warm. He put his hand against the front of her knickers and could feel the warm wetness of her body. Slipping his fingers into the front side of her knickers, he stroked the line of her pussy. He could hold back no longer; he pulled the knickers to one side, lined up his prick and entered her in one almighty push, right to the hilt. She let out a gasp as he entered her and her breathing increased along with his. He was beyond the point of reasoning now, pushing and thrusting furiously until he gave out a deafening scream as he shot into her for what seemed like for ever. He continued to screw into her for a few more seconds and she also screamed as she reached orgasm.

They lay there for a while, joined together motionless, happy and satisfied.

'That was good, honey,' Sandra said.

'That is definitely the understatement of the year,' Jack gasped.

She laughed at his humour. 'Let's go to bed,' she said.

'I'm not sure if I can make it up the stairs after that,' he laughed and she laughed with him – they both knew that the night was far from over yet.

After a few minutes' rest Jack picked Sandra up off the floor and carried her upstairs to the bedroom. It was going to be a long and special night, and he wanted it to be one that they would both remember. They got into bed and made love until the darkness gave way to the morning light and they both drifted into sleep, entwined together.

They were startled awake by the sound of a ringing phone around midday. It had been a night to remember but now Jack had work to do. He ran a bath while Sandra organised a late breakfast.

Chapter Three
The Plot Thickens

Jack finished his breakfast and headed for the nearest public phone box to ring Toot who had awoken Jack from his slumber earlier requesting a chat. Jack had taken the number of the public phone booth where Toot was calling from and said that he would ring him back on that number at 1.30 p.m.

'Hello, Toot, what's the problem?'

'No problem, Jack, just thought I'd let you know that I'm ready when you are.'

'Okay, Toot, I'll let you know as soon as I'm ready to move; it will either be today or, at the latest, tomorrow. Don't ring my home number again unless it's an emergency and if you do, then do not say anything other than giving me a number where I can ring you back. I'll ring you when the time is right. I'll catch ya later,' Jack said as he replaced the receiver.

Jack now had to find another purchaser for the other twenty-five kees; Jack had a list as long as his arm of people who would buy the goods from him but he was just starting up and he wanted to keep it simple until he found his feet. Happy Harry! Jack thought, Now there's an idea.

He went to a phone box and rang Harry's house.

'Hello, Harry, what's occurring?'

'Bloody 'ell, Jack, I didn't expect to hear your voice when I picked the phone up.'

'Life's full of little surprises, ain't it, Harry? How's business?'

'Absolutely crap, Jack, I might as well shut up shop, things are that bad.'

'Where will you be tonight? I'll be up to see you – I know it's a couple of hundred miles but it should be worthwhile for both of us.'

Harry gave his girlfriend's address to Jack and said that he'd be there after 8 p.m.; they said their goodbyes and put the phones down. Jack then telephoned Toot and arranged to meet him the following evening at 9 p.m. Jack went home and gave the car a quick check-over; he didn't want to fall victim to any breakdown that could be avoided by just a few minutes' attention. The afternoon passed quickly and after tea Jack got into his wife's car and headed south. He was looking forward to meeting up with Harry once again; they had shared many a mad moment together whiling away the hours of boredom in Parkhurst. Jack's mind wandered to some of the pranks that they used to get up to; he laughed to himself as he drove along the motorway.

Makes me wonder how we survived at times, he thought. 'Oh shit!' Jack shouted as he realised that he had just missed his turning off the motorway. Jack wondered how far it would be until he could turn off at the next exit; to his detriment it was nearly thirty miles before he could turn and head back towards the junction that he had missed earlier. He was not impressed with himself, not one iota, an extra sixty miles onto his journey he didn't need. 'I'll be late getting to Harry's now,' Jack mumbled to himself. He hoped that Harry would not think that he wasn't coming and go out before he could get there. Jack arrived at the address that he had been given just before 11 p.m. Getting lost and trying to find the address had put another two hours onto the journey. Not to worry, he thought, I'm here now and if I can sort this other twenty-five kees out then it will have been worth the hassle.

Jack walked up the path to the front door and knocked. After a minute or two a light came on in the hallway; the door opened and a tall slim girl stood there looking at him.

'Can I help you? she asked softly.

'Yes, is Harry here?'

'You must be Jack,' she said. 'He thought that you weren't coming with it getting so late.'

'Yes, I had a few problems on the way,' Jack explained.

'You'd better come in, then,' she said nervously.

'I thought you'd never ask,' replied Jack.

Jack followed the girl through another door into the lounge area and there fast asleep in the chair was Harry.

'I'll wake him up,' she said hopefully; she walked over to Harry and shook his shoulder. He groaned a little but did not wake.

'Been a long day for him, love,' Jack said, remembering how tired he was now himself. 'Here, I'll have a go.'

He walked over to where Harry was curled up in the chair and began to shake his shoulder. 'He's not dead, is he, love?' Jack said jokingly. The look on the girl's face told Jack that there was more to this than met the eye. Jack leant over Harry to shake both his shoulders when he looked down, and on the other side of the chair lay a syringe and a spoon. He picked the syringe up off the floor and looked at the girl while pointing at the syringe. Jack said one word to her.

'Heroin?'

She nodded in reply. Jack took a long look at the comatose form of Harry, then threw the syringe into the hearth, smashing it into pieces. He had one last look around the room before walking out without saying another word. To Jack, Harry was now dead – he just didn't know it yet!

Well, that was a wasted journey, thought Jack as he headed back towards the motorway and the long journey home. Jack thought about Harry and the good times that they had shared but he knew that their friendship was over.

The next day Jack telephoned Toot and made arrangements where to phone him later. He then went to speak to an old friend who had been a burglar for years but who had now retired; Jack knew that this guy had loads of bottle and would never talk if he was captured by the odd-lot. 'Hello, Pete, how's life treating you?' Jack said as Pete opened his front door. Pete was standing there with a big smile on his face.

'I heard you were out, Jack – I was going to come around to see you, but I thought I'd give you time to settle in first.'

'What are you up to these days?' asked Jack.

'Absolutely naff all at the moment. Have you got anything for me?'

'I might just have something that will suit you down to the ground.'

'What is it, Jack?'

Jack explained to Pete that he wanted him to meet up with another driver at a pre-arranged spot and exchange cars with him. The car that he would be collecting would have a hundred kees hidden in it; he would take that car to his lock-up and get the gear out. He would then collect another car from a different location and bolt a specified amount of gear under the back seat of this vehicle. He would have to do this with different vehicles until all the gear was gone, initially three cars a week but there would be more as the demand got higher.

'What do you reckon then, Pete?' asked Jack.

'I'm in, Jack, just point the way.'

'I'll organise a meeting for tonight. This first time I will come with you so that you'll know who to meet next time.'

Jack went off to find a telephone box and gave Toot a ring.

'Hello, Toot, it's me, I'll meet you tonight at 10 p.m. not 9 p.m. at Crewe railway station.'

'You are joking, Jack, it's a million miles away.'

'I've got faith in you, Toot, you can do it,' Jack laughed.

'Why a bloody railway station?'

'Because, my friend, you will be going home on a train.'

'A bleeding train! Why?'

'Because we haven't got a spare car at the moment, so we're improvising.'

'Have you got it sold, Jack?'

'Sure have, Toot!' Jack lied while wondering where the other twenty-five kee was going to go, now that Harry was out of the frame.

'Are you sure that he's coming, Jack?' Pete enquired.

'He'll be here, stop worrying, it's only twenty past ten. In this game it's always like this, always waiting for the gear or for the money. It's always waiting, waiting, waiting.'

'Does it ever run smoothly, Jack?'

'No, but that's life, Pete, innit?'

A car pulled up outside the station as though to collect a traveller. Jack flashed his lights at the parking car and the lights of the other car flashed back towards Jack. The occupier of the other car got out and made his way to Jack's vehicle; he opened the rear door and got in.

'This is Pete, Toot, and this is, Toot, Pete, and now the introductions are over, this is the situation. Pete is the one who will meet you in the future, Toot. Tonight you will return on the train and Pete, you will take Toot's car back to where we arranged. On the next meeting you will exchange cars; ours will have the money in it for this shipment and yours, we hope, will have the next lot of gear in it. Is that understood?' They both nodded their heads in acknowledgement.

'Right then,' said Jack, 'let's get going. Toot, give him the keys so that he can go ahead of me. I want to be a long, long way from that gear.'

Toot handed over the keys and Pete left them to talk while he got into the other car and headed home. 'We'll make it the same time and day next week, just a different place, eh, Toot? I'll ring and let you know where it will be.'

'Make it a bit fairer next time, Jack – halfway or thereabouts will be fine.'

'I won't be coming next time, Toot, so it can be on the moon for all I care.'

Jack walked back to the station with Toot. They said their farewells and parted company, Jack stopped twice on the way home to tell Big Dave and Rage where to leave their vehicles the following day. It had been a long week for Jack and he was pleased that he could now see something was finally coming together for his labours. He went home climbed into bed and he slept. The next morning he was up and out early; he went to a call box and rang Pete, startling him into the land of the living.

'I'll meet you in the supermarket in ten minutes.'

They wandered around the aisles of the supermarket discussing business, being careful not to be overheard, and not using actual words that would arouse any suspicions if they were. Jack told Pete where he could find the two cars and what to put in each of them and where to leave them later.

'What should I do with the other twenty-five?' asked Pete.

'Just bear with me for now on that one,' Jack said, not really knowing the answer himself. 'I'm working on it,' he said.

Pete left and went to collect the first of the two cars from a pub car park; he took it back to his lock-up and put fifty kees into Rage's banger, before taking it to a different car park and leaving it there. On his way to collect the next car he rang Jack and let him know that the first one was done. Jack then rang Rage and told him that his car had been repaired and he should collect it as soon as possible.

'Immediately,' replied Rage, sounding happy at the thought. Jack went home to await the next call from Pete.

Finally the plan is coming together; there's just the last twenty-five kee to sort out, then we'll be up and running properly, thought Jack.

A couple of hours later, Pete phoned Jack and let him know that the second one had been delivered. Jack took a drive to a different call box and phoned Big Dave with the same message: 'Your car has been repaired, can you collect it?'

'Straight away,' came the reply.

Jack returned home to relax for a while and to contemplate the movement of the other twenty-five kee. He had six days to sell it and recover the money in time for the next meeting with Toot. Jack knew that he could do it – he still had plenty of unused contacts to choose from – but he wanted to keep it close and keep it simple for now.

The next afternoon the phone rang at Jack's house and Sandra answered it while Jack was browsing through the small ads looking at the price of second-hand cars; he knew that he couldn't keep on taking Sandra's car off her. She had got used to having it at her beck and call all the years that Jack was away and he felt that he was intruding on her space, her little piece of freedom. He knew that he had to buy another motor but he didn't want anything that would attract any attention from the odd-lot.

'Jack, are you daydreaming again?' shouted Sandra.

'What's up, honey?' begged Jack.

'The phone – it's for you.'

'Right, hon'.'

Jack picked up the phone.

'Hello?'

'Hi man, it's me, Rage, do you fancy coming down to the pub for a drink?'

Jack knew that Rage wanted a meet. 'Which pub, pal?'

'The Jubilee at Pickmere.'

'See you in about an hour.'

Once again he had to take Sandra's car; she never complained but Jack felt guilty at the thought of depriving her of anything, and vowed to himself that getting another car would be a priority once this business was sorted out. Jack arrived at the Jubilee and Rage was stood outside with a pint in his hand. Jack waved him over to his car. 'What's happening, Rage?' Jack enquired.

Rage stood there with a beaming smile.

'Well, man, it's like this, it's all gone, man, and I need some more.'

'How much more?' Jack demanded.

'Ten, maybe fifteen,' Rage haggled.

'Can't do it,' said Jack. 'I can do twenty-five.'

'It's too much, man, I don't want to take anything that I can't shift, man.'

'I'll tell you what, Rage, take the twenty-five and whatever you can't sell, I'll take back. How does that sound?'

'Sounds good to me, man.'

'Okay, Rage, same deal as last time, only we'll change the locations of the pick-up and the drop-off – leave your car on the Kingsway car park tonight at seven.'

Jack contacted Pete to make the arrangements for the last twenty-five kees; he told him what to do and left him to it. Nothing more was to happen for another three days and that's when the money started to come in. Jack went to meet Big Dave and Dave handed over a bag full of money, all neatly wrapped into thousands to make the counting easy. Jack looked inside the bag then threw it onto the back seat of the car.

'Aren't you going to count it?' asked Big Dave.

'Do I need to?' Jack demanded.

'Well, no, you don't, mate,' said the stunned Big Dave.

'I'll be off for now, but I'll be in touch soon, Dave,' said Jack as he began to drive away.

'Yeah, mate, take it easy,' Big Dave shouted as the car roared off.

Jack headed for home; he was thinking that he needed a safe house to store the cash, maybe not now for this first deal but certainly in the near future. Jack would have to give it some thought. He arrived home and put the money into a cupboard – not the ideal place, but it would do for now. Jack picked up the car keys and headed for the door to go and meet Rage.

'Going out again, honey?' Sandra murmured.

'I won't be long, babe, put something on for me to eat when I get back, then we'll have an early night.'

Jack winked at her as he went out of the door; she smiled, hopeful that some unforeseen event would not occur and delay his return.

Rage had got rid of the other twenty-five kees as well. Jack was impressed with his efficiency.

'I've got most of the money here, man,' said Rage.

'What do you mean, "most"?' said Jack.

'I'm just waiting for the money off ten kees, then that will be the lot, man.'

'You've done well, Rage,' Jack said as he put the bag into the car. 'Give me a call as soon as you get the rest then I can get the next shipment organised.'

Jack took the money home and had an early night with Sandra.

'You'll have to slow down a bit, Jack, you're running around here, there and everywhere at all times of the day and night, you'll finish up having an heart attack.'

'I'll be okay, honey, I'll be okay.'

'You're not sleeping well, your brain is working overtime, you can't switch off, you need to take time out and relax.'

'Okay, honey, after this week, I will, I promise,' Jack said, not too convincingly. The next morning while Jack was having breakfast, the telephone rang – it was Rage.

'I need to see you, man,' he said with panic in his voice.

'Okay, okay, calm down. I'll meet you in an hour, same place as last time.' Jack replaced the receiver and carried on with his breakfast; he was not a man that was easily disturbed.

Rage ran over to Jack's car as Jack pulled in to the car park.

'Get in, Rage,' Jack demanded. 'What the fuck's up?'

'I'll tell you what the fuck's up,' said Rage frantically. 'I've been robbed, that's what's up, man.'

'What do you mean, you've been robbed?'

'I gave two different guys a five-kilo lay on each. One of them has paid me, the other one hasn't. I wouldn't have given it to them if you hadn't been desperate to shift the last of the gear that you had,' said Rage, while trying hard to pass the buck onto Jack. It didn't go unnoticed.

'Get to the problem, Rage.'

'This Frenchie guy from Toxteth in Liverpool, he took the gear and said he'd pay me by last night. It took me ages to track him down, then he said he wasn't going to pay me. He asked me what I was going to do about it.'

'Have you got the guy's address?'

'Yeah, man, but it's like Fort Knox, man, it's got steel doors and things, man, it's hard to get in.'

'Leave it with me, I'll sort it.'

Jack sounded like he meant it and that gave Rage some comfort; he didn't want to be the one on the wrong side of Jack. Jack went to a telephone box and rang Sandra. 'Hiya, honey, it's me.'

'How's my man?' came the reply.

'I want you to do something for me.'

'Any time for you, honey,' she said and they both laughed.

'No, not that,' Jack said while still laughing. Jack asked Sandra to get him a couple of phone numbers from the diary that he had left at home. She found the numbers and relayed them to him over the phone, while he wrote them down.

'I'll see you later, honey, love ya lots.'

'Love you too, darlin'' she whispered.

Jack rang one of the numbers that Sandra had given to him. A woman answered. 'Hello, can I help you?'

'Can I speak to Bobby, please?'

At this request the phone fell silent for a second, then an angry voice blurted out, 'Who is this?'

'Whoa, slow down,' Jack said softly, trying to defuse the situation before it got worse. 'I'm a friend of Bobby's. Who am I speaking to?'

'I'm his wife,' the voice replied.

'Bloody 'ell, Biff, I didn't recognise your voice. It's been a long time.'

'Who are you' she asked, now agitated by the fact that he knew her but she could not place him.

'It's me, Jack.'

'Jack who?' she demanded.

'Jack Dunkerley, the Norseman,' he laughed.

'Got you now,' she said, remembering the nickname that Bobby used to call Jack because he lived up north, far away from Bobby's south London manor.

'Is he there, Biff?'

'No he's not, Jack – haven't you heard? He's still inside.'

'He can't be, he must be well past his release date by now.'

'Oh he friggin' well is, only the daft bastard has only gone and knocked out one of the senior screws at Whitemoor nick.'

'Bleedin' 'ell, how much longer has he got for that?'

'There's no answer to that, they've sectioned him off under the Mental Health Act. It could be a month, a year, or even ten years.'

Jack knew that this was a ploy too often used by the prison system to justify drugging and abusing anyone who fought back at their authoritarian dictatorships; anyone who bucked the system too much got fucked up one way or another. He felt sad at the thought of this once talented man being locked in a padded cell, drugged up to his eyeballs, not knowing or even caring where he was. When he was younger he'd been one of Britain's most promising young boxers; he'd even been a sparring partner of the great Muhammad Ali for a time. He had been a good prospect until he got into life's fast lane, then he screwed up and he screwed up big time.

'Okay, Biff, I'll be in touch, take care.'

'And you, Jack, bye.'

Jack put the phone down for a second, then picked it back up again, checking to make sure that he had the dialling tone. Jack then rang another number and a gruff voice at the other end answered, 'Yeah?'

'Yeah,' Jack replied.

'Who the fuck is this?'

'It's the fuckin' tax man,' said Jack laughing, 'who were you expecting?'

'Jack... Jack fuckin' Dunkerley, ya bastard, you're a right wind-up merchant, aren't ya?'

'I wouldn't say that, BT, not at all.'

'No, you wouldn't, but everybody else would,' BT said while laughing.

'What have you got for me, Jack?'

'Who said that I had anything for you?'

'Jack, if you never had anything for me then you wouldn't have rung, would you?'

'You've got a point, BT, you've definitely got a point. I'll be at your house in twenty minutes.'

Jack explained Rage's predicament and explained that the place where the guy lived was like Fort Knox. 'We can't just do the bastard in the middle of the street because this time it's just a warning, next time, if there is a next time, it won't matter where it is.'

'You're right, Jack, we need to get in – any ideas?'

'As a matter of fact I have, I'll have a word with a guy who just might be able to do it – are you interested in the job if I can get you in?'

'Sure am Jack, especially if the price is right.'

'And how much is that, BT?' quizzed Jack.

'Well, if it was for you directly, Jack, it would be cheaper, but there's a middle man and it's really down to him, so it's got to be a grand – is that okay?'

'I'll be in touch, a grand is just fine, but just a warning for now, don't kill him... yet.'

BT laughed.

'Not yet, eh?'

Jack went to a call box and arranged to collect Pete, who he then took to Liverpool to show him the house. 'That house over there, it's got steel doors front and back and all the windows are caged on the inside – can you get in?'

'Hang on a minute, Jack, I'm retired from burgling, that's why I'm working for you.'

'I understand that, but I need a favour.'

Jack explained the situation to Pete, who then went for a walk. He came back and sat in the car, just watching for a while. 'Can you do it?' asked Jack.

'Yeah I can do it, but I'm not happy about it,' replied Pete.

'What time tonight can you be in that house for? I just want you to get in and out leaving the back door unlocked as you go.'

'It'll take time, but I'll be in and out by four o'clock.'

Jack dropped Pete off at home and said, 'Just make sure that the door is open by four o'clock, then get away from the area rapid.'

'Oh, I will, Jack, believe me I will.'

Jack laughed a little as he drove away. He stopped down the road at a phone box. 'Hello, BT, it's me, Jack.

'Hello, is everything okay?' said BT.

'Yeah, fine, we're having a party at five tomorrow morning, can you make it?'

'Yeah, I've got the address, I'll be there. See you soon.'

'Hopefully, mate,' Jack laughed as he put the phone down.

Pete arrived in Liverpool around midnight; he parked up and watched the comings and goings of people in the street for a couple of hours before feeling confident enough to make a move. He took a small bag of tools from under the passenger seat, locked the car and headed for the rear of the buildings. He entered the house next door to Frenchie's; it was just an old sash window – nothing to it, thought Pete, who was in like a flash. He made his way to the front room, trying his best not to make any noise. He could tell by looking around the house at the furniture and a lifetime's memories that the person or people living here were old; he didn't fancy the idea of someone having a heart attack on him so he took care to be extra careful – at least they weren't out clubbing and likely to return at any moment.

Pete made his way to the corner of the room near the front window; he moved the curtain to one side which gave him some vision from the street light. He moved the TV out of the way and kneeled on the floor, took a chisel from his bag and gouged a groove deep through the wallpaper and plaster of the wall that divided the two houses. It was a slow job because Pete had to refrain from waking any of the residents from either house. After a while Pete removed a brick, then another; he pushed his chisel through the wallpaper of Frenchie's house, then with his hand he tore the wallpaper gently and as quietly as possible until he could see into the room, ever-fearful that a reception committee would not appreciate his intrusion. He shone his torch through the gap in the bricks, vigilantly looking to see if he had disturbed anyone, but he was only met with silence and stillness. He quickly removed another six bricks and squeezed himself through the hole into Frenchie's house. It was only three o'clock but Pete was in no mood for hanging around and he made for the back door immediately. He had never seen a door like this one before; it had a wheel in the middle like the ones on the doors of submarines. Pete turned it slowly but surely until it clicked and he pulled it open to let himself out. He pulled it behind him, leaving it open slightly, ready for whoever was coming next, and Pete knew that he would never know who that was and Jack would never tell; he also knew that whoever was coming did not know him either and they never would. Pete felt secure in the knowledge that Jack was as solid as the Rock of Gibraltar. Pete got back to his car and sat in it for a while, making sure in his own mind that he had left nothing behind. He wiped the sweat from his brow and drove off into the night, looking forward to getting into bed and having a long sleep.

Just after five o'clock the submarine-type door was pushed open and in stepped a huge man carrying a baseball bat; he pulled a ski mask down over his face and walked through the house quietly. When he reached the stairs he stopped for a moment, looked around and listened. There was no movement, no sound, so he climbed the stairs, carefully standing on the outside edges of the stairwell so as not to cause any creaking of the old wooden timbers. He reached the first bedroom door and opened it. He went in and looked around – it was empty and looked unused. He went to the next room. The door, already slightly open, creaked as BT pushed it open further. There lying in the bed was the bag of shit called Frenchie. BT stood alongside the bed and raised the baseball bat to the ceiling, then with a mighty thud it came crashing down into Frenchie's torso, making him scream like the pig he was time after time as BT spoke to him in rhythm as he hit him with the bat:

THIS – IS – YOUR – EARLY – MORNING – CALL. PAY – YOUR – FUCKIN' – BILLS – OR – I'LL – BE – BACK.

Frenchie drifted back into a different, more uncomfortable type of sleep. BT walked back down the stairs and out of the house, making sure to roll up his ski mask to look like a bobble hat and putting the bat back into its own specially made pocket in his long coat. The same afternoon the debt was settled and Rage rang Jack to tell him.

'Eh, man, the most amazing thing has happened.'

'I know,' said Jack. 'Life's full of little surprises.'

Rage knew that it had been Jack's doing but didn't pursue it any further.

'I'll meet you at the pub later, man.'

'About half past nine, okay.'

'That'll be fine, man, just fine.'

Rage settled the debt for the final few kees and now Jack had all the money in to pay Toot. Now he could work out his profit, then he could pay Pete and BT, but he would still come out of it quite well. For Jack, he was now back to the small ads to find a decent motor, then Sandra could have her own car back on a more permanent basis. One of the ads tickled Jack's sense of humour and he had a little laugh to himself as he read it:

'For sale brilliant car, much loved baby arriving – car – baby – baby car – mmm! wife says got to keep baby. Wife – car – car – wife – car! child support agency says got to support wife bye-bye car, Tel.'

Jack was amused.

Chapter Four

The Tattooed Man

Jack gave Pete the money for Toot and told him where they would meet later that day. Pete felt safe enough driving down with the money, but returning in a different car with a hundred kees of puff hidden in the back didn't cheer him up too much. He tried to keep his mind off it by thinking about what he was going to do with his share of the money; this took away the thought and fear of being captured. Jack still had the problem of the last twenty-five kees; he didn't want the hassles of the previous escapade with the couple of no-hopers that Rage had enlisted, no this time he wanted someone who was sound and someone who could look after their own end if anything went wrong. Jack didn't mind sorting things out when necessary but he didn't want minor details to cause him more problems, especially those that would keep him away from Sandra more than he wished; he knew that she would worry about him if he was away from home a lot, although she would not complain. Jack had in mind a local guy who had moved to the west country; they had been good friends in their younger days when tearing around the town on their motorbikes. Outlaw, as he was known, stayed with the scene long after Jack had left it – he just moved to a different area.

I wonder what he's up to now, thought Jack. Surely he can't be that hard to find, he's about twenty stone and six foot five inches high, with the word 'Outlaw' tattooed across his forehead.

It was easier than Jack had thought. He went to where Outlaw's mother had once lived and the people living there now had given him her new address. After a quick call at her house Jack had all the information that he needed. Later that day, after several calls, someone finally answered the phone at Outlaw's house. 'He's asleep,' they said.

'Can you wake him?' asked Jack.

'Daren't do that,' answered the voice. 'He'll be up in about an hour or so – should I get him to call you?'

'No, I'll call him back later,' said Jack, leaving a bit of mystery to it. He called back later and spoke to Outlaw; they arranged to meet the next day at a pub on the outskirts of Jack's town. Outlaw pulled in to the pub car park in a breakdown truck. 'What the hell are you doing in that?' asked Jack.

'It's my own little business, it helps me to get by,' he replied.

'I'm amazed,' said Jack, 'bloody amazed. Have you still got that 'Outlaw' tattoo on your forehead?'

Outlaw laughed loudly, then lifted the front of his bobble hat to expose a tattoo of a bat, a bat like the ones in the Batman movies. It was right across his forehead, completely covering the old 'Outlaw' tattoo. 'What the fuck did you have that done for?' asked Jack.

'For a bet,' answered Outlaw.

'A fucking bet, you want your head examining, you crazy son of a bitch.'

'Let's get a beer, I'm thirsty after that drive. Still on the orange juice, Jack?'

'Sure am, pal.'

They went inside the pub and ordered drinks, then they found a quiet corner and chatted about old times for a while.

'How many kees can you shift in a week?' Jack asked him bluntly.

'I can do fifty a week, no problem.'

'Don't bullshit me, Outlaw, this is serious business and I don't need any more problems than I'm likely to get anyway.'

'It ain't bullshit, mate, if I tell you I can do it then I can do it.'

For the first time since he arrived he sounded serious. Jack believed him.

'I can fix you up with twenty-five kees a week for now and we'll talk again later when we've seen how this goes.'

Jack explained the system about the cars, the drop-offs, the pick-ups, the money, the whole story. 'No problem,' said Outlaw, 'but hopefully I've not come all this way for nothing. Can you sort me out while I'm here, I'll take it back myself in the truck.'

'You've got some balls, Outlaw. Are you sure?'

'Positive, my friend, positive.'

'Okay, be at Ken's hogie wagon in an hour.

'Pete, it's Jack, meet me at the corner of your street in ten minutes.'

'Okay Jack.'

Jack pulled up at the corner of Pete's street and Pete got in the car. Jack then drove off around the block, explaining to Pete where to take the twenty-five kees to and who to give it to. Pete was nervous. 'Are you sure that it's safe, Jack?'

'Safe as houses, Pete, believe me.'

Pete pulled up at the car park next to the breakdown truck; he got out and opened the bonnet of the car pretending to tinker with the engine while scanning the area for anything out of the ordinary. After a few minutes, he went to the driver's door of the breakdown truck and tapped on the steamy window. The guy inside sat up quickly and stared at him, causing Pete to take a step backwards. The window wound down slowly. 'Who are you?' asked the guy in the truck.

'Jack sent me.'

'About time too, I was falling asleep.'

'I don't mean to be funny, but can you lift up the front of your bobble hat for me please?' asked Pete hesitantly. Outlaw peeled up the front of the hat to reveal the tattoo of the bat that Jack had told him about. 'Yep, you're the right guy,' Pete said. 'Even the undercover pigs wouldn't go to that trouble. The gears in the boot of my car in a bag. I'm just going for a walk; I hope that you'll be gone when I get back.'

'Got your drift, son,' said Outlaw.

When Pete returned a few minutes later the truck had gone; he looked in the boot of his car and the bag had gone too. Pete was relieved.

I can go and sort these other cars out now, he thought as he drove back to his house. Jack could now leave the business for Pete to run; all Jack had to do was to collect the money off the buyers once a week, take his cut out of it, then give the rest to Pete so that Pete could conceal it in the exchange vehicle when he went to collect the next shipment off Toot. The next morning Jack went to look at a few cars that he had spotted in the small ads. The third car that he went to see was an eight-year-old BMW 325i in black. It wasn't too flash and it wasn't too expensive, but the main thing was that it could move like the clappers when necessary – just the job, thought Jack. He paid cash for it and left in the car with Sandra following behind in her old Ford. On his way home Jack stopped off at the Post Office where he bought two registered envelopes; he put five hundred pounds in each one and sent them both to Biff, Bobby Roberts's wife. Jack knew that she would be struggling without Bobby on the street earning and at this moment in time Jack could afford it, so what the hell. 'We've got to look after our own,' he mumbled to himself as he climbed back into his new Beemer and headed for home.

Everything was going well for Jack and it wasn't long before he had recruited three more buyers from the long list of names that he had acquired over the years; Pete was still running the show and they were now taking two hundred kilos of the best soap every week off Toot. Except for the odd week when no gear came through, it was smooth as silk, with Jack doing only the collecting of the monies so that he still kept all parties away from each other; only Jack knew the names and the faces of all the players and he was going to keep it that way. Christmas '97 was approaching and the gear was getting a bit thin on the ground; there had been a huge bust by the customs at Dover and ten tons of best soap bar had been seized. Jack was hoping that this was not going to affect his business, but it did, and in a big way, too. No more gear came through Toot for three months – Jack had to shut up shop. For the first six weeks of the drought Jack's phone had not stopped ringing; his buyers were screaming for gear and they were also under pressure from the people who bought from them. Jack was under pressure from his buyers to go and buy from another source, but the system that Jack had been working had been good to him and he didn't want to appear disloyal to Toot, even though he knew that Toot would understand the predicament. It was the beginning of March '98 that Jack received a phone call from Toot. 'Are you ready to trade?' he said.

'Give me a couple of days and I'll let you know.' Jack put the phone down, not sure whether he'd been glad to hear from Toot or not. On one hand he'd been glad of the rest and on the other hand the money that he'd earned already, although substantial, would not last for ever.

Time to get back to work, Jack thought.

The next day Jack went on a tour of public telephone boxes ringing just one buyer from each box, and having it confirmed by all of them that each was ready to begin again. Jack arranged to meet Pete at the Snake-Pit nightclub. Pete arrived in a brand new Mercedes with the full body kit – it was the business.

'Is that yours?' asked Jack.

'Sure is, Jack, do you like it?'

'Sure do,' replied Jack. 'Get rid of it.'

'What do you mean?'

'Are you fucking deaf? I said get rid of the fucking car.'

'Why Jack? What's happening?'

'We're back in business, or at least I am, and it's either the business or the car, Pete, you can't have it both ways. A car like that will only bring the odd-lot down on us like a ton of bricks.'

'It'll be in the auction tomorrow, Jack.'

'So you're back in the business with me?'

'Wouldn't have it any other way, Jack, we're a team.'

'A bloody good team as well, may I add?'

'The best Jack, the fuckin' best – when do we start?'

'I'll give you a ring as soon as anything develops, it could be any day now. Stick to the old formula, it's tried and tested, and get rid of that bleedin' car, okay?'

'Yeah okay, Jack, I'll get organised.'

'I hope so,' Jack said as he drove away.

Later that day Toot phoned Jack again. 'There's been a bit of a snag,' he said. 'There won't be anything for about a week.'

'Not to worry, these things happen, I'll let my lot know,' said Jack, not too happily, having already primed everyone to expect a delivery and knowing that they in turn would have told their own customers the same. Jack let everyone know the bad news and he apologised for the delay. There was no choice: everyone must wait – that was the name of the game, more so in this business than in most others. It wasn't long before Pete had the business up and running again and everything was mulling along nice and sweet. All Jack had to do once more was to do his weekly collections of the monies, sort out the cut and return Toot's share to Pete so that he could deliver it to Toot at the next vehicle exchange. It was some weeks later around the middle of May when Jack went to meet Rage at the usual spot to collect his funds. Jack hung around for nearly an hour before his patience expired and he left and went home. 'Any messages for me, honey?' Jack enquired.

'None today, honey, are you expecting any?'

'Not really, just hopeful,' Jack whispered under his breath.

He slipped into deep thought. 'This is definitely not like Rage. Something must be up.' Jack was noticeably agitated by the thought that Rage might have been arrested. I've got nothing here, he thought, no puff, no money, nothing written down.

Jack never ever wrote anything down about the business; he always kept it in his head, and it had only been at the start of business that Jack had kept money at his house. Now he always used a safe house that belonged to an old friend and after each deal after the cut was done, Jack would then get his mystery friend to scatter his share around several offshore companies, a couple of numbered accounts in Austria and an *anstalt* in Liechtenstein that he had long since set up, in order to avoid any seizures by the odd-lot in the event of any major disaster. Jack was determined that after what had happened to him the last time he was imprisoned, they would never take another penny from him again, ever.

Jack got into his car and went to Rage's house, driving slowly down the street to look for any signs that there had been a bust – a damaged door or door frame was usually an obvious sign of overreaction from the odd-lot. Jack parked his car some distance away and walked past Rage's house looking for clues of a raid but he could see none; Rage's car was parked in the street but there were no lights on in the house. There was no sign of life. Jack walked back up the street to Rage's house and rang the bell; he waited but there was no response.

Maybe the bell doesn't work, thought Jack as he began to bang on the door loud enough to wake the dead. After a minute or two Jack heard a noise; a door opened but it came from the house next door to Rage's. A woman poked her head out from behind the door like a glove puppet at a kiddies show.

'You won't get any answer there, love,' she said.

'Why's that?' asked Jack.

'Because he's in hospital.'

'In hospital, why?' Jack enquired.

'He's had some sort of accident. I saw the ambulance take him away – he didn't look too good.'

'Okay, love, thanks,' Jack muttered, as he walked off in deep thought, wondering what could have happened to Rage – surely he couldn't be another undercover junkie like Harry turned out to be. 'No, no, what am I thinking about? Maybe he's fallen off a ladder or something.'

Jack got back in his car and headed for the hospital. He had called Rage by his nickname for that long that it took him ten minutes to gather his thoughts and remember what his real name was; he could hardly go to the desk and ask if they had a Mr Rage in there, he mused to himself. Jack approached the desk. 'Have you got an Arthur Hawkins in here?' he asked.

'I'll just check for you, sir,' said the nurse. 'Are you a relative?'

'No, I'm just a friend, one of his neighbours said that he'd been brought to hospital, so I thought that I'd come along and see what's up with him.'

'Oh I see,' she said. 'Intensive care I'm afraid, love.'

'Intensive care?' Jack shouted. 'What's he doing in intensive care?'

'He's been beaten half to death, I'm afraid.'

'How bad is it?' demanded Jack.

'It's pretty bad. We've nearly lost him a couple of times, he's really lucky to be alive, and it's still touch and go.'

'Can I see him?' Jack begged.

'No, I'm afraid not, it's not possible at the moment, maybe in a few days' time if he's any better. He's got a round the clock police guard at the moment, just to be on the safe side.'

'Who could have done this?' Jack said to no one in particular but catching the nurse's ear.

'God knows,' said the nurse, 'but they want locking up, whoever they are.

'That's too good for them,' said Jack and meaning it too.

'Can I have your name and address, sir? I've got to have all Mr Hawkins's visitors' names and addresses.'

'Certainly, I'm John Davies of Grasmere Avenue,' Jack lied. He didn't want to be connected to anything, especially when he didn't know what was going on, and with the odd-lot on twenty-four-hour guard, Jack just wanted to slip away. He made his excuses and left saying that he would call back the next day, but knowing that he would be staying well away until the odd-lot had left his bedside. Two weeks later Jack rang the Central hospital to ask if Rage was still in intensive care, and found that he had been moved to one of the wards. A relieved Jack put the phone down – now maybe he could get to the bottom of this enigma.

'Hello, Rage,' said the angry Jack as he looked at the mess that Rage was in, even after two weeks: his eyes were still nearly shut and both his arms and legs were in plaster. 'Fucking hell, Rage, who did this to you?'

'Aaaaagh,' replied Rage. Only then did Jack realise that Rage's jaw was wired up. 'We'll get them, Rage, whoever it was, my friend, we'll get them.'

Rage nodded his head.

'Do you know who it was, Rage? Did you see anyone?'

Rage shook his head, his eyes speaking volumes in their sadness.

'If I find out who's done this,' said Jack, 'I'll do the bastards personally.'

It was two months more before Rage was allowed out of hospital and a bit longer before his memory started to return. One night when they were sitting in Rage's house watching TV, Rage just blurted out, 'Frenchie'.

'What do you mean, Frenchie?'

'That's whose voice it was, the voice I heard when I got jumped, it was Frenchie.'

'Are you sure, Rage? Are you absolutely positive?' said Jack who was now getting excited himself at the thought of concluding this matter.

'As sure as I'll ever be, it's all coming back to me, man, it's all coming back.'

'What happened then, Rage?'

'I heard a couple of motorbikes pull up outside, so I assumed it was some of my friends. I went to open the door and when I opened it four guys wearing helmets crashed in. They pushed me back into the house and started punching me; they kept asking, "where's the gear, where's the money". I wouldn't tell them, that's when I heard Frenchie's voice. He said, "I'll make him tell us, I owe him one". He kept smashing my arms, my legs, my body with some sort of club, man. I'm sorry, Jack, I couldn't take any more, I was in pain, man.'

'I know you were, Rage, I know you were – anyway, what's a hundred grand between friends?'

They both laughed, but Jack was already deep in thought. The next day Jack phoned BT and told him to take a couple of his boys with him to that same house, find the same guy and inflict some serious damage upon him, and if possible retrieve Jack's money. Jack insisted the money was secondary – serious pain was the primary objective.

Later that day BT rang Jack with the bad news. 'The bird has flown, Jack, looks like he's been gone a while. too.'

Jack had people all over Liverpool keeping an eye out for this creep called Frenchie. It was some two months later when the phone rang at Jack's house – it was Phil, an old friend. 'I've got good news for you,' said Phil.

'About Frenchie I hope?'

'Bang on the nail, Jack, bang on.'

'What's occurring then?' Jack asked anxiously.

'He's in Spain, Jack.'

'How do you know?'

'He must be getting lonely and he's phoned this chick that I know and invited her over for a couple of weeks.'

'Whereabouts in Spain, Phil?'

'Well, I know that it's Fuengirola, but I don't know the address yet. I'll let you know when I do.'

'When is the girl going over there?'

'This Saturday, she's that excited that she's telling everyone, she obviously doesn't know that he's being hunted.'

'Find out where she's flying from, Phil, where to and what time.'

'I'm right on it, Jack, I'll ring you when I find anything out.'

'Cheers, Phil.'

The next day Jack drove a hundred and fifty miles, just on the off chance that a guy would be at home when he got there, and luckily for Jack he was. 'Bloody hell, Jack, you're a sight for sore eyes.'

'You too, Max, you too.'

'You're lucky to catch me here, Jack, I only got back yesterday. I've been working on the oil rigs, got to earn a living, you know.'

'Yeah, I know,' Jack mumbled.

'I've got a month off – do you fancy coming fishing?'

'It's not for me, thanks.'

'Well, why are you here, Jack? You weren't just passing and popped in for a cuppa?'

'Do you fancy a job, Max?'

'I'm always open to offers, Jack, you know that.'

Jack explained what he wanted done and why; he also told him about Rage's injuries. Max didn't flinch; he'd seen worse in his lifetime. He'd been in the front line in the Falklands war, and after that conflict was over he went to Guatemala as a mercenary, before semi-retiring to occasional work on the oil rigs. Max was not a man to be easily frightened.

'I'll let you know when I've got more details; it's going to be soon. Be ready to move, okay?'

'Ready when you are, Jack,' he smiled. 'As long as you've got the money, I've got the know-how.'

They left it at that and parted company. The next day Jack's phone rang. 'Hello, Jack, it's me, Phil. She's on the two o'clock in the afternoon flight to Malaga on Saturday from Manchester Airport. Her name is Gaynor Gardner, she's half-caste, slim and she's about five feet ten.'

'What's the address in Fuengirola?'

'Give me a break, Jack, I've busted my balls to get this much.'

'Yeah, you're right – sorry, mate, I owe you one.'

'Don't worry about it, Jack, I'll see you sometime.'

'Yeah, cheers, Phil.'

Jack put the phone down and went out to make a call from the telephone box up the road.

'Hello, Max, good news and bad. I've got the girl's name and description, the time of her flight and the airports from and to but not the address in Fuengirola.'

'Well, four out of five ain't bad – leave the rest to me.'

Max wrote down the details that Jack had relayed to him, then he went to pack a few things for his trip – a very few things. Max always travelled light. It was Friday the next day so Max only had one working day to get organised; he went out and booked a flight for midnight and then went to a friend's office in the town centre and used his phone. He called another friend, Pedro in South America, who had relatives in Spain; they talked business for a few minutes, then Max put down the phone and thanked his friend for the use of it. He then left to catch up on some of the sleep he'd missed over the last couple of months while working on the rigs.

It was late on Friday afternoon when Max rose from his bed and stepped into the shower to waken himself to the day. Have I got everything covered, Max asked himself as he went over the details in his head. There's just a car to organise, he thought, but I can do that when I get there without too much trouble. With the normal delays at the airport and the late take-off, Max arrived in Malaga at three thirty on Saturday morning. Plenty of time to get organised, he thought as he wandered round the airport looking for a car hire booth that was open. There were plenty that had closed up for the night, but there would always be one or two that would be open continually around the clock. Max knew this, having been here on many occasions before. It wasn't long before he found a tired-looking Spaniard half collapsed over his desk in one of the car hire booths. Max hired a car – a Fiat Panda, which was the most popular of the hire cars as Max definitely wanted to blend in with the populace. Max went off to find some accommodation and found a place that he'd used before in Benalmadena – it was nothing flash but it served its purpose. Max took a shower, then got in bed to have a few hours' sleep; he didn't know when he would be getting any more for a while. Max rose at about three o'clock that afternoon, showered, then headed for the airport where he could get something to eat while he was waiting for the flight from England to arrive. The flight that the girl was on would be arriving at five thirty local time, leaving England at two and taking two and a half hours to get to Spain plus the extra hour difference in the time zones. At four thirty, Max noticed a change in the digital flight times display, and this was followed by an announcement. 'Flight E4227 from Manchester UK has been delayed and will now be arriving at 1800 hrs, a delay of thirty minutes. We are sorry for any inconvenience.' With that still ringing in his ears, Max wandered off back to the airport cafeteria to get some more coffee. He was not overly worried, as he was a patient man and he had been in worse conditions. He remembered being stuck in a foxhole for days, freezing cold, soaked to the skin and starving hungry in the Falklands, and at the other end of the spectrum when he was trapped in the tropical heat of Guatemala, dying of thirst. The comforts of Malaga Airport's air-conditioning and the hot coffee, he could cope with for an extra half an hour, he mused to himself.

Flight E4227 from Manchester eventually arrived and Max was at the arrivals gate watching the holidaymakers pass through to the airport lounge. Only two coloured girls were amongst the entourage from Manchester, the first a small stocky girl dressed half-punkish, who couldn't possibly be the one; the other one was definitely the right girl – she was tall, slim and very pretty. Max watched to see if she was going to be met by anyone as she stood outside looking around and across to the airport's car park. She waited a few moments then approached a taxi – this could be it, thought Max. The girl spoke to the taxi driver for a few minutes before getting in; the taxi drove off towards the San Miguel plant at the end of the road. Max raced across the road to where he had left his hire car; he got in and started the engine but before he drove off, he had a good look around to make sure that no one else was watching him. On deciding that he was not being followed he set off in pursuit of the taxi. Max knew that it would be heading for Fuengirola and he soon caught up with it amongst the holiday traffic. They past Aqualand on their right as they approached Torremolinos; children were still playing on the giant slides that could be seen from the road. Even now, at gone six o'clock, the sun was still shining and this was reflected by the smiling people enjoying their vacations. Max mused to himself that people always smiled more when the sun shone – it was the feel-good factor, he thought. He followed the taxi through Torremolinos down through Benalmadena and on to Fuengirola. There had been no problem following the taxi this far, but now that they were turning off the main highway, Max would have to be careful, for even if the girl was not expecting to be followed, the taxi driver may notice something suspicious and Max did not want to alert anybody to his presence. The girl was taken to the Hotel Javisol and Max, who had parked in the hotel car park, followed her into the hotel. She went to the reception desk, closely followed by Max who stood behind her pretending to be in a queue; she asked the receptionist if a Mr France had left a key for her at the reception.

'*Un momento*,' she said as she went to look. 'Your name, *señorita, por favor.*'

'Yes, I'm Gaynor Gardner.'

'*Su pasaporte por favor,*' the receptionist asked, while holding out her hand to give the naive traveller a clue to what she wanted. Gaynor handed over her passport and in return the receptionist gave her a key with a number attached to it. '*Número treinta y siete,*' the receptionist said, while pointing at the number on the key fob.

'Yes, thank you,' replied the confused Gaynor. 'Where is that?'

The receptionist pointed to the lift and to the stairway and said, '*Segundo piso, segundo piso*'.

Gaynor looked dumbfounded.

'*Segundo piso,*' repeated the receptionist. '*Segundo.*'

'Ah, second, second floor,' replied the ecstatic Gaynor.

'*Sí señorita, es correcto.*'

'Thanks,' said Gaynor as she walked towards the lift.

'*¿Qué desea, señor?*'

'*Sí, ¿cuánto es una habitación por noche?*'

Max asked how much it was for a room for one night and was given the details by the receptionist. Max had learned to speak enough Spanish to get by while working alongside South Americans in Guatemala in his days as a mercenary.

Max left it a couple of days for Frenchie and his girlfriend to settle in before he set about watching them. He booked into the hotel next door so that he could keep a closer eye on their movements. After a couple of days Max realised why Frenchie had sent for the girl – he was friendless. He may have had some friends out there at times but most people along the coast were on holiday and after a week or a fortnight they were gone again. Max looked out of his hotel window and saw the happy couple sat around the hotel pool. He then made it his business to sit next to them at the pool and befriend them both; they invited him to their hotel later for drinks but Max declined, not wishing to be seen with them in such a place where their acquaintance could be identified by the bar staff. Instead Max invited them to go to a disco with him in Torremolinos.

'I don't drink alcohol so I'll drive,' Max insisted.

'Great, I'll have some of that,' said the easily impressed Frenchie.

'I'll meet you on the car park at ten o'clock,' said Max. 'No point in going out too early, the place doesn't liven up until midnight.'

Max took them both to La Venya nightclub in the centre of Torremolinos – apparently that was the place to be, where the scene was happening, whatever that meant, thought Max. The next day he made it his business to accidentally bump into Frenchie. 'Are you coming down to the pool?' asked Frenchie.

'I can't make it today,' Max said, 'but I'll meet you tonight and we can go for a meal.'

'That'll be great, same place at ten o'clock.'

'Gotcha,' said Max as he walked away. He went off to meet his friend Pedro's cousin who was also called Pedro. Pedro worked for the Spanish equivalent of the Mafia, smuggling hashish from Morocco into Spain; his cousin from Guatemala had spoken to him and asked him to help Max in any way possible and so he was more than helpful. He arranged for the things that Max needed and told him to call him if there was anything more that he could do or if he needed any assistance. The next morning at about five o'clock, when Jack was dropping Frenchie and Gaynor off at the hotel after a night out dining and dancing, Max invited Frenchie out that same day to go sea fishing. 'I can borrow a boat and we can have a few hours on the sea,' he said.

'That'll be great,' shouted the drunken Frenchie.

'I'll pick you up at four o'clock at the bus station,' said Max, now deep in thought. They all went off to get some sleep after the night's events had drained their energies. Max set his alarm for one o'clock, jumping out of his bed when it rang and getting straight in the shower to freshen his body for the day. He dashed out of the hotel without eating and went straight down to the marina at Benalmadena. He found Pedro waiting for him there with the boat that they had arranged; it was more like a yacht than a fishing boat but it would do the job. Max and Pedro went on board for a while and had a long chat which culminated in them standing on the quayside shaking hands and promising to meet again some time in the future. Max went to collect Frenchie from the bus station where they had arranged to meet earlier. It was only when Max arrived at the bus station that he realised that Frenchie was bringing Gaynor with him – there would have to be a change of plan, he thought. They greeted each other warmly, like old friends, but Max never lost track of why he was there and what he was there for. Max was a professional to the core. He drove the three of them down to Benalmadena marina and parked quite some way from the yacht.

'Follow me,' Max said as he headed for the boat and the three of them marched along the quayside.

'Is this it?' asked Frenchie.

'Sure is,' replied Max.

'This isn't a boat, it's a bloody liner!' joked Frenchie.

'It's beautiful,' said the stunned Gaynor.

'Let's get aboard or we'll be here all day,' teased Max.

'Whose are those bloody dumb-bells?' Frenchie asked as he climbed on board. 'You'd have to have arms like Schwarzenegger to lift them up, they must weigh fifty pounds each.'

'Must come free with the boat,' joked Max. 'You wouldn't get me weightlifting.' They set off and headed out of the harbour into the choppy waters of the Med; it was calmer the further that they got out to sea, and soon the sight of land disappeared into the distance. They were an hour and a half out to sea in the Straits of Gibraltar when Max dropped anchor and got the fishing equipment out. He showed Gaynor where everything was in the galley so that she could prepare a meal, and then took a bottle of wine on deck to Frenchie who had set up a couple of the rods and was now happily watching the lines from his deck chair in anticipation of a catch. Max went back downstairs to one of the cabins; he opened the safe and took out the Beretta that Pedro had left for him, and the 9mm ammo that he had specially prepared himself earlier and loaded the clip of the weapon. He left the cabin and walked back through the galley, passing Gaynor on his way through. As she turned to let him pass, he grabbed her around the neck in a commando-type hold while putting one hand over her mouth to muffle any scream that she may let out. It was over in a second; her neck was broken and she was dead in his arms before he lowered her to the floor. Max walked back up on deck; he casually walked up to the half asleep Frenchie and put two rounds into the back of his head. Frenchie slumped to one side and slipped onto the deck of the boat. Although there was blood pouring from the body, it was not as much as there would have been if Max had used normal bullets; he had purposely used soft-tipped rounds so that none of the bullets would pass through the body and out of the other side. The soft-tipped rounds would bounce around inside the body wrecking everything in their path until they came to rest; they would not leave the body causing another visible wound.

Max carried Gaynor's body from the galley and laid her onto the deck of the boat. He handcuffed her to one of the dumb-bells and then he handcuffed Frenchie to the other one. He then rolled, dragged, and pushed both of the bodies off the boat into the deepness of the sea.

Max raised the anchor and headed back to mainland Spain, dropping anchor again just off the coast of Marbella. He put the dinghy over the side in the darkness and secured it to the yacht with a rope; he went down into the galley, making sure that all the windows were locked and the deck hatches were secure. Making the galley watertight, he then connected two pieces of fuse wire to a battery, one piece to the positive and one to the negative – the other ends he then wired to an alarm clock, which was set to go off in half an hour. Before leaving the galley Max turned the Calor gas stove on without lighting it, allowing the gas to seep slowly out into the galley; he then left, closing the hatch as he went. He clambered onto the dinghy and started the 10hp motor up, cutting through the rope that attached it to the mother ship like an umbilical cord, and made for the street lights that he could see glowing in the distance. Max left the dinghy on the beach and walked up the long path to the top of the cliff. He sat there for a while looking out over the immense ocean, waiting in anticipation of the event to come, then out of the quietness came a loud bang, followed instantaneously by a huge fireball which lit up the ocean for a few minutes before disappearing back to darkness, swallowed up by the ever-hungry sea.

Max looked down to the key in his hand that he had taken from Gaynor's body; he looked at the key fob – number thirty-seven was written on it. The job was not over yet, he thought to himself. Max walked into the centre of Marbella and took a bus back to Benalmadena to collect his hire car. Later that night he entered the Hotel Javisol via the back staircase and made his way to room thirty-seven; he went in and packed all the belongings of Frenchie and Gaynor plus seventy grand that was stashed under Frenchie's bed, hidden in an old suitcase. 'Fucking amateur,' Max uttered under his breath.

At least this money will be of interest to Jack, thought Max as he loaded all the bags together near the front door. He gave the place a quick wipe over before he left – even though his hands were gloved he couldn't be too careful. Max carried the bags down the back stairway to his car, then he drove back to his own hotel to get some sleep – it had been a tiring day.

The next day he dumped the property of the now deceased pair at a local rubbish tip, scattering the items amongst the tons of other rubbish that was dumped each day. He got rid of all the items except for the seventy grand that he'd found which was now in his hotel room awaiting transferral to a safer place. Max spent the next couple of days resting before checking out of the hotel and heading for Andorra, up in the mountains between France and Spain. He had a numbered bank account there and the seventy grand would be better there than trying to explain its presence to the British customs if he was stopped on his way back through at Manchester airport.

The following week Max was back in England and he had arranged through Charles to meet up with Jack. Jack didn't mind the drive down to Max's house if he had time and the business was going all right, which it was in Pete's ever more capable hands. Jack still only had to sort the money out once a week and of course keep all his contacts in the shadows, so that none of them ever met.

'Come in, Jack,' Max said while greeting his friend with a firm handshake.

'Did you sort it, Max?'

'Is the Pope Catholic?'

'Job done then?'

'Yep, job done.'

'So now there's just your fee to sort out.'

'I've been paid, Jack, I paid myself out of the seventy grand that I found in Frenchie's hotel room.'

'You found what?'

'Seventy grand in cash.'

'Fucking hell, thanks to that bleedin' amateur we've had a right touch!'

'You've had a right touch, Jack. Froghead has gone to feed the fish and you've got most of your money back, except for my modest fee of course. Where do you want the rest transferring to? I've got it banked.'

'You keep it, Max, you've earned it. Look on it as a bonus, I do.'

Jack laughed; he was glad that this particular scenario was over. Max never mentioned that the girl was dead too, and Jack never asked. They said their goodbyes for now and Jack drove back to the motorway and headed for home. He was feeling quite pleased with life; this little episode had ended satisfactorily, and the other business left in Pete's hands was running smooth. He could now take things easy, to Sandra's amazement.

There was another message at Charles's house for Jack to ring a girl called Shirley. Jack rang and said who he was. A woman's voice said, 'Hang on a minute.'

'Hello, Jack,' the man's voice said.

'You're not Shirley,' said Jack.

'It's me, Bernard, ya daft teg.'

'And I thought my luck was in,' laughed Jack. 'What can I do for you, Bern?' he enquired.

'I need a chat, Jack, when is the best time for us to meet?'

'How urgent do you need to see me?'

'Reasonably.'

'How about the day after tomorrow at two o'clock at The Mucky Duck?'

'I'll be there,' Bernard said as he put the phone down.

Jack took Sandra out for a meal.

'What are we celebrating?' she asked.

'Nothing in particular, honey,' said Jack, not wishing to discuss the facts of the last few months' business and the fact that he'd saved fifty grand without having to pay Max out of his own pocket, as he would have had to if the money had not been recovered. It all made for a pleasant experience for Jack, and when he was happy Sandra was happy too. They were like two lovesick teenagers – they held hands everywhere, they were forever kissing each other, and at home Sandra was always sat on Jack's lap, hugging him, never wanting to let go of him and him not wanting her to. They were happiest when left in their own company together, away from the ills of the world.

Bernard turned up on time and looked eager to talk business.

'Not here,' said Jack, 'there's too many people about. We'll go to my car.'

They sat in the car at the edge of the Black Swan car park. The Black Swan was known to locals as The Mucky Duck, although Bernard was not a local he knew this place from his previous meetings with Jack over the years.

'What's so urgent then, Bernie?' asked Jack.

'Five million dollars, Jack.'

'What about five million dollars?'

'I can get hold of five million US dollars, and I want half a mil. Sterling for them, in legit notes if you please.'

'How good are they?'

'They're fucking good, Jack, they're the best. They've not all got the same serial number like some that are going about. These have got two thousand different numbers amongst them. We've tried them at the bank and they've taken them, no problem.'

'Well if they are good enough for the Bank of England then I should be able to find a buyer, half a mil you say gets 'em five?'

'You've got it, Jack.'

'I'll ask some people that I know and see what they say. By the way, who's paying me?'

'I'm paying you, Jack – you're in for a hundred grand if you can do the business.'

'Get me some samples and I'll see what I can do.'

'I'll give you a bell as soon as I can arrange it.'

'Whenever you're ready, Bern.'

Bernard left Jack's car and went back across the car park to his own. Jack watched Bernard drive off before leaving the car park himself.

Chapter Five

Storms Ahead

Two weeks later Jack hired a camper van and took Sandra and their daughters on a fleeting tour of Europe. He used the holiday not only to have a break with his family but also to do a personal check on his foreign bank accounts, and to meet one of the lawyers who was running an *anstalt* for him in Liechtenstein.

Unbeknown to Jack, back in England thunderstorms were rife, causing floods in some areas. Jack's problem was not the floods but the lightning which had struck his house causing the burglar alarm to go off. The security firm that Jack was wired to had a van there in minutes and two guards checked that the property had not been entered, then radioed back to their control room to see if they had the name of a key holder who could come and reset the alarm. The control room contacted Jack's brother Charles who was the only name on the list of key holders. Charles came out to turn the alarm off but every time that he tried to reset it, the alarm would go off again immediately. After several attempts, the now not very amused Charles decided to leave the alarm turned off until the next day when he could get the alarm company out to fix it. He telephoned the security company and explained the problem; the control room of the security company radioed through to the guards in the van and asked them to keep an eye on the property, if and when they were passing it during the night.

Charles arrived the next day to let in the man from the alarm company. Only when they entered the lounge did he realise that something was amiss, the TV and video were noticeable by their absence. Charles went cold at the thought that he had been the one that had decided to turn the alarm off.

Maybe I should have left it ringing all night. What the fuck is our Jack going to say, he thought. The man from the alarm company fixed the alarm and then Charles secured the property, boarding over the broken bathroom window where the burglar had entered and resetting the alarm before he left.

Later that evening and purely out of the blue, Jack rang Charles to see if there had been any messages for him, and Charles explained to him what had happened. As usual Jack was not flustered. Worse things had happened to Jack in his lifetime – a few bits of property that could be replaced was not the end of the world.

'The main thing for now is not to let Sandra know just yet. Ring Steve Donoghue and get the TV and video replaced,' said Jack.

'Okay, I'll sort it out. By the way, when are you coming back?'

'I'll be back in a couple of days.'

'Okay, I'll see you then,' said the relieved Charles as he replaced the receiver and then immediately picking it up again and dialling. 'Hello, Jackie, is Steve there?'

'Yes, I'll just get him for you, he's buried under tons of computer parts at the moment, you know what he's like.'

A few moments later Steve came to the phone.

'Hello, Charles, what can I do for you?'

Charles explained what had happened to Jack's house and that the TV and video needed replacing before Jack arrived home with Sandra and the girls.

'Leave it to me, Charles, I'll give you a bell tomorrow and you can let me in to the place.'

'No problem, as soon as you're ready, Steve.'

A couple of days later Jack pulled up outside his house.

'Have you had a nice break, honey?'

'Lovely, Jack, absolutely lovely.'

'I'm glad about that but there's a bit of bad news to come,' he said.

Sandra's heart sank as she demanded, 'What bad news?'

Jack explained that they had been burgled and that he hadn't wished to ruin her holiday by telling her before and there would have been nothing they could do about it anyway. Sandra grabbed her keys and rushed towards the house, closely followed by Jack and the girls; when they got inside Sandra noticed immediately that the TV and video had been exchanged even though the two items that now took their place were the same models. Sandra knew the difference, she knew every line in the wood-grain of her own TV – after all she had polished it everyday for almost a year since it was bought; the same as she did with everything in the house each day. By anyone's standards she was house-proud to the point of being obsessed. Sandra ran around the house checking to see if anything else was missing or at least noticeably missing; everything else seemed to have been left untouched.

'Must have been a burglar in a hurry,' said Jack, 'or someone without transport, maybe it was kids.'

It was late by the time Sandra had cleaned the house from top to bottom; she felt that the house was unclean, that 'they', the intruders, had raped her. She took it personally, whereas Jack did not; he wasn't happy about being a victim but he understood that every man had to make his own way through life and it wasn't for Jack to tell any man how he should do this. The exception was if the burglar knew Jack and took advantage of the fact that he knew that he was away for a few days to line his pockets. This he would take personally, but he could think of no one that he came into contact with that would have the nerve; and if any of them *did* find the nerve, then they would have emptied the house and not just taken the TV and video.

Later when Jack and Sandra were just about to get into bed, Sandra jumped up quickly climbed onto a chair and searched desperately on top of the wardrobe like a woman possessed.

'Jack, have you seen my jewellery box anywhere?' she said, as tears began to run down her cheeks as the truth of the situation finally sank in.

'I've not seen it, honey. I thought that you took most of the stuff with us on holiday.'

'I did, but there was that chain that I got from my grandmother left in it and a few cheap trinkets. I'm not bothered about the other things but I can't replace the chain; it's not very valuable in money terms but the sentimental value is priceless,' she cried.

She was beyond consolation at this time; Jack just held her in his arms and lifted her from the chair, her fruitless search now over.

Early the next morning they were woken by a loud banging on their front door. Jack looked out of the window and first noticed a police car parked in his drive; looking down towards his front door he then saw a uniformed police officer. Jack motioned that he would be down momentarily; he then picked up his dressing gown and put it on as he walked down the stairs, closely followed by Sandra. He opened the door and looked at the policeman without speaking.

'I'm here about the burglary,' he said.

'What burglary?' asked Jack.

'You did have a burglary here recently, didn't you?'

'Not us, not here. Where did you get your information?'

'From the alarm company.'

'There must be some mistake,' said Jack. 'It was lightning that set the alarm off, there was no burglary here.'

'Okay if that's the way that you want it,' said the cop.

'That's the way I want it,' replied Jack.

The cop walked away towards his car, stopping only for a second to look up at the boarded bathroom window. Sandra said nothing; she knew that Jack was not a great lover of the police at the best of times. She respected his view that the police were a necessary evil; she also knew that eventually Jack would sort out any problems in his own way.

The disturbance of the policeman knocking on the door and the sound of voices had awoken Jack's daughters who came down the stairs in need of food and drink. They all sat around the kitchen table and had some breakfast. Jack then lazed in the bath for a while. The phone rang in the distance and it was answered by Sandra; she shouted upstairs that it was for him.

'Ask them to phone back in fifteen minutes,' said Jack, quite miffed at having to leave the comfort of his hot bath. He got out of the bath and got dressed. He had just reached the lounge when the phone rang again.

'How's the telly and vid?' said Steve Donoghue.

'Fine, Steve, just fine, how much do I owe you?'

'Well, er, ah,' then he laughed.

'You didn't phone me to ask about my health, did you?'

'Well, not exactly,' he laughed again.

'I'll come to your house later when I'm passing and sort it out with you. Thanks for the stuff anyway.'

'You're welcome.'

'Cheers.'

They put the phones down and Jack took out his phone book and rang a few numbers, asking people to find out about the burglary at his house and asking them to keep an eye out for Sandra's chain – it was stamped 'Manchester 1922'. Jack put the phone down and started to play back the tape from his answerphone; there were plenty of messages that had accumulated while he had been away, most of them from Bernard wanting Jack to ring him urgently at Shirley's. He went to a phone box and rang Shirley's number.

Bernie answered, 'Where the fuck have you been Jack? I must have rung you a million times.'

'I've been on holiday.'

'You've been on holiday? I thought you'd left the planet – it's easier to find gold on the streets of London.'

'I didn't want to be found.'

'Okay, okay, point taken, when can we meet?'

'Mucky Duck at two tomorrow.'

'See ya then.'

'Yeah bye.'

And the phones went down.

Bernard was in the car park when Jack arrived; he walked to Jack's car and got in.

'Have you got the samples, Bern?'

'I've had them for nearly two weeks. I've been walking around like a nervous wreck.'

'Yeah, I know, I've got a full tape of you on my answerphone,' Jack laughed.

'Will you be able to do the business?'

'I'll let you know,' said Jack as he started the engine of his car and Bernard got out. Jack sent the samples to a chemist friend to be tested. If they pass his tests then I'll show them to the 'A' team, Jack thought. It was almost a week before he got the thumbs up on the dollars. He then rang John who was one of the 'A' team and arranged a meeting for the following day. He was up early the next day and drove for nearly three hours to get to the meeting. Jack discussed the five million dollars and gave John the samples to take away; they made arrangements to meet again when there was more to discuss. Jack took the long road home, deep in thought about the business in hand.

Two weeks later and Jack had still not heard from the 'A' team; he wasn't sure if that was because the dollars were not up to scratch or if the team were just organising getting the half a mil together. He had no doubt that the 'A' team had the funds but like his money it was probably sat in banking institutions around the world and some may even have been tied up in major cannabis deals. God only knows, thought Jack.

The phone rang.

'Hello, Jack.'

'Hello,' said Jack. 'I recognise the voice but I can't put a face to you.'

'It's Harry,' said the voice. 'Harry the fence.'

'Bloody 'ell, Harry, it's been a long time, it's no wonder that I couldn't place your voice. What can I do for you?'

'It's what I can do for you, Jack.'

'And what's that, Harry?'

'Manchester 1922 – ring any bells, Jack?'

'Where are you living these days?'

'Same old place.'

'I'm on my way,' said Jack as he picked up his coat and raced out of the house towards his car.

'I thought that we were having a night in together,' Sandra shouted across the drive.

'We are, honeypot, we are, something's cropped up. I'll be back in half an hour, promise.'

'Don't I'll-be-back-in-half-an-hour me, Jack Dunkerley. I know your half-hours.'

'Believe me, honey, I'll be back.'

Jack arrived at Harry's dilapidated terraced house with its rundown garden, and knocked on the door. A dog barked on the other side of the door. 'Down, boy, get down,' bellowed out Harry's voice from inside the house. The door opened and Harry stood there with his hand twisted in the collar of the now frothing beast. 'It'll be okay, Jack, come in.'

Jack walked into the house that had a distinct smell of dog kennels. It didn't concur with his nostrils.

'Sit down, Jack.'

'Not much time,' said Jack, lying, but not wishing to sit on the flea-ridden sofa or offend the owner. 'What do you know about this chain?'

'I've got it here.'

'Let me see it.'

Harry went to another room and returned with the chain – it was Sandra's.

'How did it come into your possession, Harry?' Jack demanded.

'Hang on a minute, Jack, I didn't burgle your house.'

'I know that, you're too fat, you wouldn't have got through the window,' Jack said, half-laughing.

'Very funny,' said the offended Harry. 'I bought the chain off a guy.'

'How much do I owe you, Harry?'

'I couldn't take money off you for your own chain.'

'How much did you pay for it, Harry? I won't ask again.'

'A oner.'

'A hundred quid,' Jack said as he took a wad of notes from his pocket, counted out a hundred pounds in tenners and gave it to Harry.

'Cheers, Jack, but I still feel a bit uneasy about taking the money from you.'

'We all have our own ways to make a living, Harry. I might not agree with yours and you may not agree with mine, but we've all got to feed our families and you can't hold anything against a man for doing whatever he's got to do to earn a crust.'

'That's a fair point, Jack.'

'One more question – who robbed my house?'

Harry stared at Jack for a minute, long and hard, not wishing to say anything, but he saw a coldness in Jack's eyes that could freeze a pond on a summer's day. Harry went to his desk, took out a pen and a piece of paper, wrote down a name and address and gave it to Jack.

'You never got it from me, Jack,' Harry begged.

'You can be sure of that,' Jack said as he left.

He then went home for his night in with Sandra; after they'd eaten and Sandra had drank a couple of glasses of wine, Jack teased her that he had a present for her in his pocket. She ran to his coat and retrieved the missing chain. She was ecstatic, dancing around the room with joy, the whole four feet ten inches and eight stone of her glowing with delight at the return of her precious chain.

'I love you, Jack Dunkerley,' she shouted.

'I love you too, darling,' replied Jack. They kissed passionately for a few moments, then Jack picked her up and carried her off to bed; she snatched up the bottle of wine as they went by it and took it with her to the bedroom.

The next morning Jack rang his long-time buddy, Davie 'O'. Davie and Jack went back a long way to when they were in their teens before going on to work together as nightclub bouncers for nearly two decades.

'Hello, Davie, what are you doing today?'

'Not a lot, what have you got planned?'

Jack explained to Davie about the burglary and that he'd retrieved the chain and that he was now going to pay a visit to the burglar and would Davie mind coming along.

'What do you want me to do?'

'Just come along as a bit of back-up in case there's a welcoming committee,' Jack laughed.

'I'm in,' laughed Davie. 'What time are we going?'

'Best make it early evening. I can't see many burglars being up early in the morning. I'll pick you up around five o'clock.'

'I'll be ready.'

Jack walked up the path of the house, closely followed by Davie. He double-checked that he had the right address from the piece of paper in his pocket, then knocked on the door. A tall, skinny, spotty man answered it.

'I'm looking for Bill Smethwick,' Jack said politely.

'That's me,' answered the guy, who had hardly got the words out of his mouth when a clumping right hand from Jack sent him sprawling backwards into the house, quickly followed by Jack, who was just about to punch him again when he looked around at where the sound of a scream had come from and saw a woman and three children sat on a sofa and another young boy sat next to them in a wheelchair. They were all huddled around a small portable TV; the whole family looked mortified as Jack rushed in. Two of the children began to cry, closely followed by a third. Jack never had the heart to punch the burglar again in front of them; he picked the guy up off the floor and directed him into the kitchen, where they could talk.

'Do you know who I am?' asked Jack.

'No idea,' said the now terrified burglar.

'I'm Jack Dunkerley.'

'I've heard of you.'

'It was my house that you robbed the television and video from and a chain that is irreplaceable to my wife, a chain stamped "Manchester 1922".'

'I can get the chain back for you,' he stuttered as his whole life passed before his eyes with the realisation of who he'd burgled.

'I've already got the chain back – where's the rest of the stuff?'

'Gone,' said the guy not wishing to grass up his buyers. Jack admired him for that and never pursued the issue. The burglar went on to explain that the social security only gave him a pittance a week to live on and he couldn't make ends meet, with a wife and four children to feed, one of whom was wheelchair-bound.

'A man can't let his family down, he can't just sit there and watch them starve – you've got to look after your own.'

Jack couldn't argue with that – he'd been saying the same thing for years.

'You just be careful who you're robbing next time,' Jack said as he began to leave. 'Just one thing, how did you know which house to burgle?'

'My mate has got a scanner and while we were listening to it, we heard some alarm company control room telling some of their guards to keep an eye on the property because the alarm had been turned off.'

'Technology, eh, bloody technology,' quipped Jack. 'One more thing, how much did you get for the chain?' he asked on a hunch.

'Fifty quid,' replied the burglar.

'A man's got to make a living,' Jack smiled to himself at the thought of Harry the Fence having got one over on him. He wasn't too worried about the loss of a hundred pounds – after all it had made Sandra happy. Jack walked back into the other room where the other children and their mother were sat with Davie 'O' still blocking out their exit route. Jack could see fear in all their eyes and he felt a twinge of guilt; it was not his intention to frighten women or children. He looked around the room and apart from the portable TV and the sofa they had nothing – no carpets, no basic necessities and certainly no luxuries. Jack doubted that there would have been food in the cupboards if he had looked. On his way through the house as he was making his way out, Jack took a wad of notes from his pocket and gave it to the little boy in the wheelchair; then, without looking back he left the house, gathering Davie 'O' who had watched the events with some amusement.

'You must be going soft in your old age, Jack.'

'Maybe, my friend, maybe.'

It was another week before John from the 'A' team rang Jack and arranged another meeting. It seemed like a good sign to Jack; hopefully the deal would be sorted out and then the pestering Bernard would stop harassing him to death. He met John a few days later and discussed business. John wanted Jack to arrange for the five million dollars to be dropped off with him; he then wanted the seller to wait for a week before getting paid their half a million. Jack said he'd see what he could do.

'No fucking way, Jack,' Bernard shouted while almost having a heart attack.

'Why not, Bern?'

'How do I know that I won't get ripped off?'

'Because they're friends of mine, and what else are you going to do with the dollars if these boys don't take 'em?'

'I don't fuckin' know, Jack, I don't know.'

'Well when you do, let me know.'

'Listen, Jack, how about if we get half the money up front?'

'I can ask them, Bernie, but don't hold your breath.'

Jack spoke to John and explained Bernard's fear; he then came back to Bernard with another offer.

'A hundred grand up front, and that's the best that you're going to get.'

'Okay Jack, at least it's something – if the job goes boss-eyed at least we're not left skint.' Jack and Bernard then made the arrangements for the transfer of the dollars to London, where John soon had them redistributed to his contacts around the world. Within days Jack had been paid the other four hundred thousand pounds, a hundred for himself and three more for the ever-pestering Bernard.

'Thanks Jack, you've done me proud.'

'One does what one can, Bern.'

'I'm off for now. I'll be in touch.'

'Don't make it too soon,' laughed Jack.

Bernard laughed too, not quite understanding what Jack had meant by that last statement, and not wishing to ask.

Chapter Six

A Drop in the Ocean

Pete telephoned Jack.

'Hello, Pete, what's happening?'

'Nothing, that's the fucking problem.'

'You don't sound very happy.'

'I'm not, mate, I'm as sick as the proverbial parrot – when can we have a chat?'

'I'm tied up today, will tomorrow be okay?'

'It'll have to be, where at?'

'Come over to my place around noon.'

'I'll be there,' Pete said as he dropped the phone, disengaging the line.

He arrived at Jack's and was welcomed into the house. Jack took him through to his 'office' – it wasn't really an office, just another room of the house where Jack could have some peace and quiet without being interrupted. When they had sat down, Jack rang through to the kitchen on the internal phone.

'Two coffees to the office please, love.'

'Do you think I'm your slave or something?' Sandra ranted.

'Usually,' laughed Jack, causing the conversation to lighten.

'I'll bring some through shortly, *sir*,' she jested.

Pete explained that there had been no cannabis delivered to them for weeks; Jack already knew this as he hadn't been to collect any funds since the drought started. Pete said that he was worried that the drought would continue for quite some time.

'What do you want me to do about it?' asked Jack.

'I've got an idea.'

'Then let me in on it, Pete, I'm always interested in good ideas.'

'Well, Jack, you've got the connections around the world, why don't we bring our own in?'

'Our own what?'

'Our own cannabis shipments.'

'That is not a good idea. We should leave that side of it to the professionals – we should stick to what we know best.'

'But it's the so-called professionals who are letting us down and in turn we are letting our own customers down. If we had our own direct supply, we'd be able to supply our customers constantly, while at the same time maximising our profit margin.'

'I'll think about it and get back to you. You've raised some good points.'

Sandra entered with the coffee.

'Will there be anything else, sir?' she said while doing a little curtsy.

'Not at the moment, miss,' Jack said as Sandra left the room.

'What the fuck was all that about?' asked the bemused Pete.

'Just a private joke,' Jack laughed.

Coffee and business over with, Jack and Pete parted company. Jack went to find Sandra and took her by the hand.

'Excuse me, miss, but there will be something more after all,' Jack grinned.

'And what might that be, sir?' she said as she was led to the bedroom by Jack. 'Oh sir, you don't mean, you can't mean!'

'Can't mean what?' asked Jack mischievously.

'Well, sir, you've brought me to the bedroom, so that can only mean one thing.'

'And what might that be, miss?'

'It's pretty obvious, sir.'

'Is it, miss?'

'Yes, you want me to empty the chamber pot.'

They both laughed, fell into each other's arms and had some long-overdue sex. Jack got out of bed first.

'I'll put the kettle on while the bath's running,'

'Good idea,' said Sandra as she rolled herself up in the quilt. Jack returned with a cup of tea for her.

'How do you fancy a holiday, honey?'

'I'd love one, Jack,' smiled Sandra. 'Where to?'

'I thought somewhere hot, like Spain,' Jack replied while his mind wandered to a plan he was thinking of.

'It would be nice, honey, but what about the girls and school?'

'The girls won't be coming, your mother is going to look after them.'

'Oh, that's nice, when did you ask her?'

'You haven't yet,' Jack laughed.

'She might not want to.'

'She will if we pay her.'

'Well, she's always open to bribery,' said Sandra.

'It must run in the family,' laughed Jack.

'Cheeky pig!' Sandra shouted as she threw a pillow across the room at the now mobile Jack.

The following weekend, the couple flew from Manchester to Gibraltar. Jack collected his hire car, then drove through the border checkpoint that separates Gibraltar from Spain. As soon as he crossed into Spain he was in La Linea where his old friend Whisky Joe lived. Joe was a giant Moroccan who had an appetite for whisky only dwarfed by his own size. Jack found that Joe was out on his travels around the town and knew that it would be an impossible task to find him. He left a message at Joe's villa that he would be back the following day. He hoped that he had made himself clear to the girl who was there; he wasn't too sure as she just continually nodded at him without uttering a word. Jack then drove with Sandra to the hotel that they had previously booked in Marbella some forty minutes drive away. He had purposely booked a hotel some way from Joe's villa, so that he could travel to Joe's to talk business but still be far enough away to let Sandra enjoy her holiday without too much interruption.

'*Amigo, amigo, amigo,*' Joe shouted as Jack walked towards his villa.

'Hello, Joe, it's been a long time.'

'*Mi amigo*, where have you been?'

'I've been around, Joe, I'm always around,' Jack smiled.

They went inside Joe's villa and talked business. There would be no problem organising the gear, Joe told him; the only problems that he could foresee would be that he would need a substantial sum of money up front for that amount of gear and the only other problem was that his people would not bring it into England. Jack would have to organise a boat to meet the yacht at some predetermined spot off the coast. When Jack had gleaned all the information that he needed from Joe, he said his goodbyes and went to finish his holiday with Sandra, where they sunbathed, swam and toured the Costa del Sol during the days, and wined and dined away the warm nights, until it was time to return to Britain and the children that they had both so desperately missed. It had been a productive trip for Jack; not only had he gained an extra holiday but he also now had a plan to put to Pete, who still hadn't had a shipment from Toot.

'If I can get some gear shipped in, have you got somewhere to stash it, Pete?'

'How much gear, Jack?'

'A ton,' said the smiling Jack.

'I can soon find somewhere,' said the now excited Pete. 'When will it be?'

'Three weeks' time, if everything works out okay.'

'I'll get it all sorted. I'll organise a stash and something to cart it in, leave it to me.'

'I don't want to know where it is.'

'Gotcha Jack.'

Jack went to see Rage.

'What's happening, mate?'

'Absolutely fuck all, man, since I got that beating and you cut my supply off.'

'What choice did I have? The odd-lot knew that the beating wasn't over nothing – did you want to finish up in the nick as well?'

'They weren't watching me, man.'

'You mean you couldn't see them watching you, which makes it even worse. Believe me, Rage, they were there, and I couldn't afford for you to lead them any further. Anyway, we give you a nice pension, didn't we?'

'Yeah, man, it was really good of you, man, but it's not the same, man, I miss the buzz.'

'Then I've got a proposition for you, Rage.'

'What is it, man?'

Jack explained to Rage that he would have to purchase a large rib (inflatable boat) and he would at a certain date have to sail to a certain spot off the coast to meet a yacht from Spain.

'I can do that, man, yeah, I can do that.'

'You'll need someone to help you, and make it someone who doesn't know me.'

'Yeah, okay, I've got someone in mind, he's an okay guy.'

'I hope so, Rage, for your sake.'

Jack flew to Gibraltar for the weekend and finalised the arrangements with Whisky Joe; on his return he told Pete when it would be coming in. He then had to fly out to Europe and meet up with Whisky Joe in Liechtenstein to organise the funds; Joe was willing to take two hundred and fifty pounds per kilo up front and the rest if and when it got through to England. Jack withdrew two hundred and fifty thousand pounds from one bank and Whisky Joe deposited it in another; then with the deed done and the arrangements made they both headed back to their own countries to sort out their own end of the deal.

Jack gave Rage the money to purchase a rib, making doubly sure that he understood not to buy a fluorescent orange one which was the norm but to acquire a black or dark blue one. He told Rage where the meeting with the yacht was going to be, the time, the position and the date; all Rage had to do was get there and wait.

Jack told Pete to take his camper van and go down to Conwy in north Wales and keep an eye on what Rage and his partner were doing; then once they had set off for the meet, Pete was to wait and make sure that they got back all right, safe from the sea and without them getting nicked.

Pete watched as Rage and his friend Padge set off from Conwy and headed out to sea. They followed the coastline until they got off the coast of Cornwall some hours later; the sea was still calm and they headed further out until they got to the meeting point twelve miles out. They turned off the engine and drifted for a while, then started the engine again to get back to the same spot. They did this numerous times while waiting for the yacht to appear.

'I don't think anyone's coming,' said Padge.

'They'll be here,' said Rage with some optimism.

It was six more hours before the yacht appeared and by then the sea had turned rough; it was a task to keep the two vessels close enough to load the rib.

'We're going to have problems with this weather,' Rage said to the guy on the yacht. 'Let us take half of the gear now and come back for the rest later.'

'Fuck off,' he replied. 'If you think that we're going to hang around here for twenty-four hours, you must be fucking mad.'

'Okay, okay,' said Rage, 'keep it coming, we'll take it all.'

They kept loading until the whole ton was on board; it was more bulky than Rage and Padge had imagined it was going to be. The rib bobbed about in the rough water as the yacht turned and headed out to sea. Rage had trouble starting the engine and they had been pushed along at quite some pace by the fierce rolling sea; even with the engine running the rib was only making slow progress through the strong currents, and every time that the propeller came out of the water in the now very rough sea, the engine would cut out. This was a safety measure built into the engine but for Rage and Padge it didn't make them feel very safe at all; by the time that they had restarted the engine each time they had been pushed further and further out to sea.

After a couple of hours of this ever-repeating series of events the rib ran out of fuel, and panic set in with Rage and Padge. They were out at sea in the pitch blackness of night in force gale stormy seas, and not only had they run out of fuel, but they also couldn't call the coastguard for help because they had a ton of cannabis on board, which they didn't think would go down too well with the local judiciary. They hung on for another half an hour when Padge was so seasick that he thought that he was going to die. The rib was being tossed about so much that it almost turned over and they lost some of the twenty-five-kilo bags of cannabis overboard.

'We're going to die,' said Padge, horrified at the thought.

'I know, man,' said Rage, thinking that one way or another his number was up.

'I can't take any more,' said Padge while spewing his guts up all over the vessel.

'Neither can I, man,' said Rage as he fired a flare up into the darkness far above them. He then got on the radio screaming, 'Mayday, Mayday!' and giving his location using the coordinates given by the GPS system.

'Hey, man, help me to get this gear off the boat.'

'I'm too ill.'

'You'll be much worse tomorrow, if you're sat in Exeter prison on remand looking at a ten stretch.'

Padge crawled across to the stash and they both began to throw the twenty-five-kilo packages overboard; they had only just got rid of the last package when they were rammed by a customs vessel which wrecked the rib. The coastguard arrived seconds later and pulled the two men to safety on their lifeboat, while the customs towed the rib back to the harbour at Newquay. The two men, although frozen and wet, were stripped and searched by the customs on the harbour side. One of the men, Padge, was later taken into hospital with hypothermia. Rage later heard one of the customs men talking to one of the coastguards. 'What were you doing out there?' said the coastguard.

'We heard the Mayday and as soon as we heard it was a black rib, we were suspicious.'

'But these guys weren't doing anything wrong.'

'There wasn't anything on the rib when we got there, but they were up to something.' Rage had explained to the customs officers that he'd set off from Conwy earlier in the day to do some sea trials on the rib that he'd recently bought. Rage and Padge were both kept in custody for two days, before being released without charge.

The hard bit is yet to come, thought Rage. Jack will never believe that I threw a ton of best soap bar overboard, never to be seen again.

Meanwhile a frantic Pete had been close to having a nervous breakdown; when Rage and partner had not returned to Conwy, weird thoughts were going through his head – maybe they've nicked the gear, maybe they've drowned, or maybe they've been captured. Pete's mind was working overtime and he'd rung Jack numerous times already; he rang him again in desperation, only this time Jack said that he knew where they were. Pete packed up his belongings and headed out of Wales. He arrived at Jack's house some hours later and Jack explained the situation to him.

'They threw a ton of best soap into the sea.'

'Yeah, they sure did.'

'Are you having that?'

'Well, the customs have seized the rib, so I can assume that since they are not in custody any longer, that there was nothing suspicious like a ton of best soap on the fucking thing.'

'Fucking hell, Jack, I'm sorry.'

'Not as sorry as me, but such is life, so let's learn from it. We're not importers, we're distributors, let's stick to what we know best.'

'Mmm, when we can get the gear you mean.'

'It's waiting for you now, I've had a call from Toot.'

'Right then, Jack, I'll be off to sort things out.'

'Yeah, you do that, Pete,' Jack said as he walked him to the door.

The next evening Rage went to a call box and rang Jack.

'I'm sorry about that catastrophe, man.'

'It's not your fault, Rage, shit happens, and sometimes it happens big style.'

'What are we going to do about it?'

'What can we do about it. Absolutely nothing, but it will be best if you don't call or see me for a while, because you'll be a target for the odd-lot for quite some time.'

'I get your drift, man. Take it easy and I'll catch up with you at some later date for a chat.'

'Sure thing, Rage.'

Jack put the phone down and sat there for a while wondering what idea he could come up with to recover the quarter of a million pounds that he'd just lost. He stayed there for a while, finally falling asleep in his armchair.

Chapter Seven

The Long Firm Connection

Some weeks later, Jack received a phone call from Frank Crawley, a man that he had known for many years, although he had not seen or heard of him for some considerable time. They arranged to get together the following Saturday afternoon at Henry's wine bar in Manchester.

'Nice to see you, Frank.'

'And you, Jack, it's been a long time.'

'Yeah, time flies, dunnit?'

'Yep, sure does,' Frank shouted across the table to Jack as the noise of the crowd muffled out their voices.

'We'll have to go somewhere quieter,' shouted Jack with his hands over his mouth like a megaphone. Frank nodded and proceeded to leave, closely followed by Jack.

'It was bleeding noisy in there, Frank.'

'Wannit just, mate?'

'Where should we go?' asked Jack.

'There's a cafe in Kendal's store that's reasonably quiet at this time of the day.'

They wandered across the road into the rear of Kendal's. They ordered coffees and sat down to talk. Jack asked Frank if he could put him onto any good scams, as he'd just lost a big chunk of his pension fund in a bad deal, and he was looking to recover his losses in whatever way that he could.

'Have you ever thought of setting up a long firm?' asked Frank.

'What's a bloody long firm?'

'It's like this, Jack – you set up a company, then from that company, you order and pay for goods from several other companies, increasing your order each time; then when you've built up a bit of trust with them, you then apply for a line of credit, usually thirty days, then you hit each of the companies for the biggest order that you think that they'll deliver, and then, my mate, you do a moonlighter. It's easy, Jack, we've been at it for years, we've had millions.'

'It's interesting, Frank, but it's not for me, thanks all the same.'

'Well if you change your mind, and you need a hand, you know where to find me.'

'Yeah, like I say, thanks anyway.'

Jack got up to leave, when Frank said, 'You don't know where I can get some gear do you, Jack?'

'What sort of gear?'

'Puff, draw, cannabis, call it what you like.'

Jack sat back down and whispered, 'What are we talking, ounces, kilos, or tons?'

'Kilos, Jack, maybe a hundred a week, if the price is right.'

'The price will be right, but who's buying? This isn't your sort of graft, Frank.'

'I've got these guys, businessmen, who've been pestering me for ages, I've got the odd kilo here and there for them, but they're now looking at getting involved in a bigger way, and they're looking for someone who can deliver a hundred kees a week, regular.'

'How safe are they?'

'I've known them for years. I've done loads of business with them in the past without any problem.'

'If you can get them to put half the money up front, then I'm interested, but only because you guarantee these people; there are too many snitches around these days to take chances.'

'I'll have a word with them, Jack, and see what they think. If you give me a ring in a couple of days I'll let you know what they say.'

Jack left it almost a week before ringing Frank back to ask him how he'd got on with his associates.

'They won't have it, Jack, they say that they've been had before, so they won't risk it.'

'Well I suppose that it was worth asking, eh?'

'It's always worth asking. There is one thing – they said that they are willing to do a straight exchange, cash for gear if you can arrange it.'

'I can arrange it, but I'm not going to, it's far too dangerous.'

'What d'ya mean, dangerous?'

'I mean it's too on top, I don't even know these guys.'

'No, but I do, they're as safe as houses. I've done business with them before. Just think about it, will you?'

'Okay, I'll think about it.'

The next day Jack mentioned to Pete that someone wanted a straight change over deal, cash for gear.

'I don't fancy that much,' said Pete.

'No, nor do I,' Jack agreed.

Following some weeks of harassment by Frank, Jack approached Pete again.

'Listen Pete, Frank's been on my case again. He's like a pit bull with a postman when he can smell money. Anyway, he's promising that if we do the deal and it goes all right, then this firm that he's dealing with will definitely take a hundred kees every week and they'll use our system. What do you think, Pete?'

'I don't like it, but I'll chance it just the once. If they're going to take a hundred every week then my wages might go up too,' he laughed nervously.

Jack arranged to meet Frank two days later.

'How's things, Frank?'

'So so, Jack, you know how it is, but these guys are driving me mad over this deal – can you sort it?'

'It's sorted, Frank. Where do they want to meet for the exchange, and make it somewhere local.'

'I thought the Swan car park, as it's on the edge of town, and it's handy for the motorway too.'

'That'll be fine with us. Sunday at half seven – that gives both of us three days to get organised. What car will your man be driving?'

'He'll be driving a red Transit van. I'll ring you if there's any change in the plan.'

'Don't ring me otherwise,' Jack said firmly.

Jack told Pete what the plan was, and explained that Pete had to meet up with a guy who'd be in a red Transit van in the Swan car park on Sunday evening at seven thirty.

'I'll sort it out,' said Pete.

At a quarter to eight on Sunday evening, Jack's phone rang; it was Pete complaining that there was no sign of a red Transit at the meeting place. Jack told him to hang around for a while, then replaced the receiver. No sooner had he done this when it rang again.

'Hello, Jack, it's Frank. My man has just been on the phone, telling me that your guy has not turned up yet.'

'That's odd, because my man has just rung, and told me that your man hasn't shown up.'

'They can hardly miss each other in that car park – it's only big enough for about eighty cars.'

'Yeah, you're right, but something's wrong. Are you sure that your guy is in a red Transit?'

'Sure, I'm sure, I don't know how your guy can miss him – there can't be many Indian guys sitting in a red Transit van on that car park.'

Jack went cold.

'What's the Indian called?'

'What difference does it make?'

'It makes a lot of fucking difference. What's he called?'

'He's called Patel.'

'Saleem Patel, and he's aged about thirty?'

'Yeah, do you know him?'

Jack cut him off and rang Pete's house where Pete's girlfriend answered.

'If Pete calls, tell him that Jack said that he's got to get away from where he is and go home – he'll know what I mean.'

Jack put the phone down and shouted to Sandra, 'Something crucial has come up and I've got to nip out for a while. I want you to stay by this phone, and if Pete rings, I want you to tell him to get away from where he is and go home – he'll know what you mean.'

Jack drove to the Swan and parked on the road outside, avoiding having to venture into the car park. He went inside the pub using the side entrance, went to the bar and ordered a drink. He could see across the bar into the lounge area on the other side, where there were at least a dozen men trying not to be conspicuous while at the same time watching the car park from the uncurtained windows. Jack spotted the Indian stood amongst them; he also recognised at least one of the odd-lot and his blood ran cold. Jack slipped back outside unnoticed and got into his car; there was no way that he could get to the car park to warn Pete. Jack had a terrible sinking feeling in his stomach – after all Pete didn't even want to do this job and he'd only given in to pressure from Jack, the same way as Jack had let Frank talk him into it. If only Frank had mentioned that his connection was an Indian before the deal was set up, Jack thought. He went to a phone box and rang Pete's house, but the phone was engaged, as it was each and every time that he rang it all through the night.

'Come to bed, Jack, it's six o'clock, and you look knackered,' pleaded Sandra.

'There's a good reason for that – I am knackered – but I won't be able to rest until I know what they've done to Pete, what they're charging him with, and which nick he's going to be kept in. He won't get bail with that much gear.'

'There's nothing you can do now, so get a couple of hours' sleep, then you'll be able to think a bit straighter.'

'Maybe you're right.'

Jack fell asleep as soon as his head touched the pillow; Sandra lay there looking at him, stroking his brow, and worrying about what sort of trouble he might be in. He was woken by Sandra at ten o'clock; she'd brought him a cup of tea. 'I didn't think that you'd want to stay in bed all day,' she said.

'No, you're definitely right,' he replied as he struggled to get dressed and drink his tea at the same time. He had a quick wash then dashed downstairs and out of the house to the phone box up the road and rang Pete's house. His phone was still making the engaged tone.

'There's definitely something wrong,' Jack said out loud to himself. He then drove down to the magistrates court and went inside; there were a few cases listed for that day, but even if Pete was to be in this court, his name wouldn't be on the list as he'd only been arrested the night before, and the list had probably already been up for a week. Jack asked the usherette if there was to be any extra cases that day other than what was on the list. She replied, 'Definitely not.'

Jack then assumed that the police would be keeping him in the cells for the maximum period possible to see if they could get him to talk; there was nothing more that Jack could do, so he went home to wait.

Twenty minutes later he was fast asleep on his chair. He was awoken three hours later by the ringing phone.

'Hello, Jack.'

'*Pete*. Where the fuck are you?'

'I'm at home.'

'Meet me in half an hour at the Kingsway pub.'

'Yeah, okay, Jack.'

Jack had a quick shower to freshen himself up, and then he went to meet Pete at the Kingsway. Jack was ten minutes late, and Pete was sat there amusing himself with a pint of Tetley's Best.

'What's going on, Pete?'

'What do you mean?'

'I mean, what happened last night?'

'Absolutely fuck all.'

'Don't give me that bollocks. I saw police all over the fucking place.'

'What are you talking about? There weren't any police anywhere near the place.'

'Listen, Pete, I saw the fuckers, and now I'm smelling a rat.'

'What do you mean?'

'I mean you wouldn't go hookie on me would you, Pete?'

'That's an insult, Jack. I thought that we were mates.'

'So did I, Pete, but you can't blame me for getting paranoid when I saw the police looking out of the side windows of the pub at the car park, where you were parked with a hundred kees of best soap bar.'

'Yeah, I was there, but there was no red Transit and definitely no fuckin' police, and now I think about it, there were no fuckin' windows overlooking the car park.'

'Are you fucking mad?' Jack said angrily.

"Course there are windows overlooking the car park, I've looked out of them hundreds of times.'

Then something dawned on Jack, a sudden realisation that caused half a smile to cross his face.

'Where were you at half seven last night?'

'You know where I was, I was where you told me to be.'

'And where was that?'

'I was at the Mucky Duck.'

'You jammy, lucky bastard,' shouted the now laughing Jack. 'When I said the Swan, I meant the Swan on the outskirts of town, not the Black Swan. If I'd meant the Black Swan I'd have said the Mucky Duck. You were lucky, Pete, it was a set-up, and we nearly came unstuck – you don't know just how fucking close it was. And, anyway, where've you been all night?'

'Well I was that pissed off when no one turned up, that I went home, took the phone off the hook and went to bed.'

'You went to bed, and I've been up all night worried to death that you'd been nicked.'

'Funny old life, Jack, innit?' said the grinning Pete.

'You can say that again.'

'Anyway, what's the idea of your mate setting us up?'

'No, you've got the wrong idea there. Frank never set us up, he was just a middle man trying to earn a shilling on the deal; he wouldn't have known that the Indian was working for the odd-lot. That fucking Indian nearly had me again.'

'What do you mean again?'

'It's a long story, Pete – maybe some other time, eh?'

'Whenever, Jack.'

'Listen, Pete, I'm sorry that I thought you'd gone hookie on me, but in my position you'd have thought the same. I thought you'd been nicked with a hundred kees and then the next thing is you're sat in the pub with me. You can't blame anyone for getting paranoid over that, can you?'

'I suppose not, when you think about it.'

'Anyway, let's get back to business.'

'Yep, and let's stick to our own system, fuck going to jail if we can help it.'

'I'll second that, Pete, any day of the week.'

They finished their drinks and left to go to their respective homes and on with the business of distribution.

Chapter Eight

Indian Uprising

Jack had put the word out that he wanted to trace Saleem Patel, and that he was also willing to pay a small fee to anyone who may have some useful information, such as where he was hiding. It was going to be a difficult task finding the Indian; Jack knew that he could disappear from one Asian community and reappear in another many miles away without causing so much as a ripple. The Asians were renowned for looking after their own kind as so often happened with minority groups. Jack knew that while he was waiting for what could turn out to be a very long time, he had to get on with the cannabis business and replenish his pension fund.

With the passing of the summer months Jack's arthritic shoulder started to remind him that he was no longer a teenager. He had suffered with arthritis in his shoulder for many years; in the cold weather it would make itself noticeable with increasing pain. Jack thought that working in draughty nightclub doorways had created the problem in the first place, and now that he had it, he found the recurring problem a nuisance. It was only September and Jack was not looking forward to the cold winter months ahead.

'I think that we should buy a villa in Spain and sit out the coldest three months of the year in the Mediterranean sunshine – what do you think, Sandra?'

'Sounds like heaven to me – should I pack now?' she laughed.

'Maybe not this minute, but soon, I think.'

That same week Jack phoned one of the agents and arranged to view some properties. One week later he and Sandra were in the airport lounge at Manchester when Jack noticed a man looking at him, then turning away when he caught his eye.

'Sandra, that guy over there, the one in the leather jacket and jeans, do you know him from anywhere?'

'I don't think so, honey, should I?'

'I seem to know his face from somewhere, but I just can't place it.'

Just then an announcement came over the tannoy system.

'Will all passengers for flight number GW1747 to Malaga please make their way to boarding gate number eight.'

Jack and Sandra boarded the aeroplane and awaited take-off. Sandra never did like the initial take-off procedure; once that she was in the air she was all right, but getting off the ground in that catapult-like motion was somewhat of a trauma for her, and she held on to Jack's arm for dear life. Jack always liked to sit close to a window and look down onto the clouds; he thought they looked like giant bales of cotton wool, soft and beckoning. He would often stare out of the window into the nothingness and let his mind wander into daydreams. This time, however, his daydream was short lived as the air hostess leant over Sandra and dropped the folding table down from the seat in front.

'Would you like anything to drink, sir?' she asked.

'Coffee please,' Jack answered as she finished pouring Sandra's and began to pour one for him.

'Would you like a meal, sir?' she asked while holding out a small plastic container, which Jack took from her.

'Yes I think that I could manage one of those, how about you, San?'

'Me too,' Sandra replied.

Jack opened the container to find a couple of salad sandwiches cut into triangles and some cheese and crackers; after eating it, he turned to Sandra and said, 'That's made me hungry. I could do with a meal after that.'

'Shush,' said the embarrassed Sandra, 'they'll hear you.'

'I hope so,' said Jack, 'then maybe they'll bring me some more.'

'Men!' said Sandra under her breath.

Jack got up to use the toilet at the rear of the plane; when he returned he said to Sandra, 'There's a guy back there in a red tee shirt. I'm sure that he's the guy who had the leather jacket on in the airport lounge, the one who was staring at me.'

'He might have been, but what's wrong with that?'

'I don't know, I just seem to know his face from somewhere.'

'Maybe it will come to you.'

'Yeah, maybe.'

Jack and Sandra collected their luggage and wandered through the green Nothing to Declare route towards the arrivals gate. As they walked through the corridors into the airport's main building, Jack noticed a man holding aloft a large card with 'Mr J Dunkerley' written on it. Jack approached the man.

'I'm Jack Dunkerley.'

'I've been sent by Lamptons estate agents to collect you, and take you to your hotel, courtesy of Ms Smallbonks.'

'Thanks,' Jack said while laughing to himself at the Spaniard's mispronunciation of Ms Smallbanks's name. The driver dropped Jack and Sandra off at their hotel and told them that a rep from Lamptons would meet them there the next day.

'Hello, I'm Susan, from Lamptons.'

'I'm Jack and this is my wife Sandra.'

'I believe that you are looking for a property around the Marbella area?'

'Yes that's right, but not so close that we can't escape the hustle and bustle.'

'We have a few properties around Estepona; the area is much improved since the new mayor was voted in a few years ago. What sort of property are you interested in?'

'To be honest we're not sure, that's why we're here, to have a look around.'

'Well we've got a selection of apartments available at Las Terrazas de Bel Air, a standard block with balconies overlooking a pool and with views of the sea and mountains. Prices range from £59,000 for a one bedroom to £120,000 for a three. Also we have a luxury villa called El Velerin, traditionally built with whitewashed walls and red roman tiles. The entrance hall has a spectacular vaulted ceiling and antique full height doors, making simply entering the house something of an event. The price for this one is £495,000.

'Sounds nice,' said Sandra.

'There's more to come yet,' said the rep.

'What else have you got in that area?' asked Jack.

'There's the Adorna Tierra, a spectacularly ornate villa, fitted with glass crystal everything, crystal chandeliers, crystal table tops, even crystal door knobs – and as for the bathroom, well,'

'And how much is that?' asked Jack.

'About £2.2 million.'

'Phew!' Jack whistled.

'We do have one a bit cheaper, further towards Marbella, very handy now that the new inland road is built. It's Valle del Sol at San Pedro de Alcantara, a bit more modest, but possessing some charm, with round bays topped with conical roofs. It's priced at a cool £1.2 million.'

'Very modest,' said Jack sarcastically.

'Which would you like to see first?'

'I think that we should see all of the ones that you've mentioned – what do you think San?'

'Good idea, Jack, it'll give us an overall view of things.'

'Let's go then,' said the rep, as she led them out of the hotel to her car.

After they had travelled a few miles, Jack noticed that they were being followed, but he said nothing about it to the two women. All through the afternoon from one property to the next, he was aware of his pursuer's vehicle parked in the distance. Jack racked his brains about the guy who he had seen on the aeroplane, the same one who he'd seen back at the airport in Manchester; then, like putting the last piece into a jigsaw puzzle, the picture was clear – the guy in the leather jacket had also been one of the men looking out of the windows of the Swan pub awaiting the arrival of the accidentally elusive Pete. He had been stood amongst Inspector Graylor and his men, so what was he now doing two thousand miles away from home following Jack?

When they got back to the hotel, Jack told Sandra that they were being followed and had been all day.

'Something stinks, San,' Jack said while drifting into thought – 'I'd better not contact Whisky Joe on this trip.' When the rep from Lamptons called to collect Jack and Sandra the next day, she was told that they had already left. By the time the rep had got to the hotel, Jack and Sandra were already back in England. Jack rang Lamptons and apologised for having to leave so suddenly; he also told them which of the properties that he was interested in buying and said that he'd make arrangements for the purchase of it through his lawyer in Liechtenstein. Jack had been home from Spain a few days when he told Sandra that he was nipping out to see Pete. 'I'll be back soon,' he said as he left the house and walked to his car in the drive. Jack met up with Pete and sorted out their immediate business, then he dashed home to Sandra. He was looking forward to a night of passion with her while their daughters were staying with their grandmother. Jack arrived home to a quietness that was unusual in itself; he wondered what exotic delights Sandra had in store for him. As he wandered through the house towards the lounge he shouted, 'I'm home,' but there was no reply. Jack laughed to himself, thinking that Sandra was playing one of her little games; he walked into the lounge and was taken aback by the welcoming committee – there were five guys stood in his lounge. Three were Asians and two were white guys; one of the white guys was holding a gun to Sandra's head. Jack was not impressed. One of the Asians, the older one, was known to Jack.

'What's going on here,' Jack demanded.

'Calm down, Jack,' said the older Asian.

'You enter my property and hold a gun to my wife's head, and you want me to calm down!'

'I just wanted to get your attention.'

'Well, you've certainly achieved that,' growled the angry Jack.

'Let's have a private chat in the other room, Jack,' said the older Indian.

'And leave my wife in here with these baboons?'

'It won't be for long.'

'Tell your monkey to get that gun away from my wife's head.'

'Who are you calling a fucking monkey?' said the man with the gun.

'Fucking hell, a talking monkey,' Jack said sarcastically.

'I've heard of you, Dunkerley, but you don't frighten me, you're getting old,' said the gunman.

'That's a fact, but if you'd like to put that gun down, I'd like to see if you fight as much as you talk, you big-gobbed tosspot.'

The old Indian interrupted the arguing men, and told the guy to move the gun from Sandra's head. Jack then led the older Indian through to another room, but he was not happy with the thought of leaving Sandra to fend for herself in the other room with the Indian guy's heavies. The Indian told Jack that he'd heard that he was looking for his son Saleem and that he knew what it was about.

'You know what it's about?' said Jack.

'Yes I know,' said the Indian.

'Well you tell me what you think it's about,' demanded Jack.

'A few years ago my son Saleem was arrested with three kilos of heroin. One of the police that nicked him was an Inspector Graylor. The inspector, for reasons best known to himself, offered my son a deal where if he could implicate you, then he would face no charges himself. He couldn't face the thought of going to prison, so he did a deal with them by getting me to ring you and asking you to drop some money off for this girl. I didn't know at that time that he'd done a deal with the police but it was easy to figure out later. And again recently Graylor put pressure on him to help him to get you once again.'

'I know, and this time he failed.'

'Yes he failed, but he'll try again – why does he harass you so much?'

'First of all so that he could get at my wife; he thought it would be simple if he got rid of me, but he was wrong – she wouldn't have anything to do with him. So now he's on a mission to destroy me, but he won't succeed.'

'Listen Jack, I know that you can be a dangerous man, but you're also a compassionate man – try to find it in your heart to forgive my son. I have much money, name your price?'

'Name my price, what for? All the suffering that I had in prison all those years for something that I hadn't done, all the suffering that my wife and children have gone through while I wasn't there to comfort them.'

By this time Jack was striding up and down the room; then he stopped and sat on the arm of a chair.

'I'll have to think about it,' he said while pressing the button on the silent alarm with his foot.

'You don't have much time, Jack, you'll have to tell me now.'

'Maybe I don't want to tell you now.'

'Your wife is in the other room with some serious people, Jack – let's not let it get out of hand.'

'It's already out of hand,' snarled Jack.

He sat there staring at the Indian guy for a few minutes when there was a banging on the door. Jack went to answer it. As he got into the hallway, the white guy with the gun ran out of the lounge, and told him to stay where he was, but the older Indian guy stepped out of the other room and told the white guy to hide the gun.

'Answer the door, Jack,' said the Indian.

Jack opened the door to find three security men stood there. 'Your alarm went off at our control room, is there a problem?'

'Not yet, but these guys are just leaving,' said Jack smugly.

'Very clever, Jack,' said the Indian. 'Okay, you men, let's go. I'm sorry that we didn't work something out, Jack, I really am sorry.'

'I'm not,' said Jack.

As the Indian and his men trooped out of Jack's house, the guy who'd held a gun at Sandra's head turned to him and said, 'We'll meet again sometime, Dunkerley.'

'You can bank on it,' smiled Jack.

'What was the problem?' asked one of the security men.

'Just a difference of opinion,' answered Jack. 'Thanks for coming – it stopped things getting out of hand.'

'You're paying the bills, mate,' he laughed as he walked away.

'I suppose I am,' said Jack as he closed the door.

He walked back into the lounge where he found Sandra in tears; she threw her arms around him and said, 'I thought that they were going to kill us.'

'No, they had no intention of killing us, otherwise we'd be dead already. There's no use in wanting to talk to someone if you're going to kill them anyway; he just wanted to save his son's skin. He was hoping to buy me, but he knew that he couldn't before he got here.'

'Why did he come then?'

'Two reasons, the first being that he had to try something to save his son.'

'And the other?'

'Yes, the other, that's a different story. He came to look into my eyes; he was searching for a glimmer of hope.'

'And what did he see?'

'Only death, pain and heartache.'

'How do you know?'

'I know, believe me I know.'

A few days later another Indian, Saed, had heard that Jack's wife had been threatened, and he didn't agree with this sort of treatment to women, so he tipped Jack off about where the other Indians were hiding. Jack rounded up a crew of heavies and at three o'clock in the morning, they crashed the door in at the Indians' safe house. There were no men there, only three women – one older woman who spoke little English and two younger ones who said that the men had fled the country. Jack was not amused that his prey had flown the nest. He telephoned the local airport to see if they had any flights to India and they did not; Jack then rang the London airports, only to find that the two men had left on an earlier flight to Bombay.

'Were they on return tickets?' Jack asked.

'I'll just check, sir,' said the receptionist. 'No sir, just one-way, I'm afraid.'

Jack put the phone down; he was deflated at the thought of the Indians escaping his grip. One day, he thought, one day.

Two weeks later Jack had a call from Davie 'O'.

'I don't know how true it is, but there's a rumour going around that the guy who pointed the gun at your wife is a doorman called Arthur from the Cherry Tree pub. Apparently he's been bragging about it to all and sundry.'

'When is the place open again? I'd like to take a look at him.'

'It's open every night, but he probably only works at weekends.'

'Okay, we'll take a look at the weekend. We'll just look for now, and we'll sort it later.'

'Whatever you say, Jack.'

The following weekend, Davie 'O' and Jack sat in the car park of the Cherry Tree pub, watching as the staff arrived for work. They had been sat there for a while when an old Cortina pulled onto the car park and two doormen got out.

'That's him, Davie, that's the bastard.'

Jack went to get out of the car when Davie said, 'I thought you were just going to weigh the situation up.'

'I was until I saw that bastard; he's the one who had a gun to my Sandra's head. I'll do the bastard.'

'Whoa, Jack, keep calm.'

'I am calm, Davie.'

'Listen to me – this is his turf, and we don't know if he's tooled up. We're not prepared for this. Leave it for now and come back another day, now that you know where to find him,' Davie pleaded.

Jack got out as the two men walked towards the pub's main entrance.

'Hey, bollocks,' Jack shouted at the top of his voice. The two men looked around. 'Yes, I'm talking to you,' he challenged.

They looked at each other then walked back towards the car park.

'We meet again, Dunkerley,' one of them said.

'Yes, only now the terms are more equal.'

'We've got three more men inside the pub,' the doorman said.

'Yeah, well there's two of us, and two men should be able to handle five young boys.'

'You're too old Dunkerley, you'll get hurt.'

'Well if I'm too old, then you won't mind a straightener round the back will you, just you and me?'

The guy took his coat off and proceeded to walk to the rear of the pub. Jack gave his coat and his watch to Davie 'O' and followed him. Davie 'O' and the other guy's mate agreed to follow the two men, but just to watch the fight, not to get involved.

The two men squared up to each other, the younger one dancing and jabbing, while Jack conserved his energy. Jack took a few jabs to the face and was beginning to wonder if this had not been one of his better decisions; he caught the other guy with a couple of weak jabs that had little or no effect. The other guy's confidence lifted, and he threw a lunging left jab at Jack, which Jack blocked effectively; he also kept hold of his opponent's arm with his left hand, while grabbing his hair with his right hand. He then ran the gunman's face along the rough bricks of the pub wall, tearing the skin from his face as he went. There was blood everywhere. Jack was banging the other guy's blood-soaked head into the wall and his opponent's friend tried to intervene.

'I wouldn't do that if I was you,' said Davie 'O', as he slipped a knuckleduster onto his hand in full view of the other spectator. Jack continued to smash Arthur's head until he was in a state of unconsciousness; he then broke both of his opponent's arms, and the two spectators cringed as they heard them snap. A breathless Jack then turned to the other doorman and said, 'Tell him not to pick on old men in future.'

He waved to Davie 'O' and they walked back to the car.

'You're getting worse in your old age, Jack,' Davie laughed.

'Davie, I'm knackered. I'm definitely getting to old for this game, but I'd do it time and again if anyone threatens or touches my Sandra or my daughters.'

There was a police siren screaming in the distance.

'Can you hear that, Jack?'

'Sure can, mate, let's get out of here.'

'Someone in the pub must have seen the fighting.'

'What fighting? I was at home all night with my wife.'

'Yeah, me too,' said Davie as he threw the knuckleduster out of the car window into a hedgerow.

Chapter Nine

Land for Sale

Charles was in his office at the skip yard when there was a knock on the door.

'Come in,' he shouted.

A man entered the room and spoke.

'Hello, Charles.'

'Hello, Nick, what can I do for you?'

'I'm looking for your Jack actually, is he around?'

'He doesn't come down here much these days – I run this business for him. I can ring him and get him down here if it's important.'

'Oh, it's important all right,' said Nick.

Charles could see that Nick was distressed, but he didn't want to pry into his business, so he dialled Jack's number.

'Hello, Sandra, is Jack there?'

'I'll just get him for you.'

'Hello, Charles, what's happening?' enquired Jack.

'I'm at the yard, and Nick is here; he seems pretty distressed, and he wants to talk to you.'

'Tell him I'll be there in half an hour.'

Jack then shouted to Sandra who was in the kitchen, 'I'm just nipping out, love, I'll be back later.'

'Okay, honey, give me a ring when you're on your way home, and I'll put your tea on.'

'Yeah right, see you later,' Jack shouted as he headed for his car.

Jack walked into his old office at the skip yard.

'Hello, Charles, everything all right?'

'Yeah fine.'

'And what's with you, Nick?'

'Can I have a private word with you, Jack?'

'I'll just go and check the wagons over,' volunteered Charles.

'Yeah, good idea,' said Jack.

Charles left the room and closed the door behind him.

'What's the problem, Nick?'

'Well, Jack, it's like this – a few weeks ago my eight-year-old daughter was sexually assaulted by some weirdo. The guy's a nutter – he shouldn't have been on the street in the first place, all this care in the community is a load of bollocks. Anyway, this guy has been in custody since he was arrested, that is until yesterday when he was released without charge. The Crown Prosecution Service say there isn't enough evidence on its own and they don't want to put an eight year old through the trauma of going in the witness box at a crown court trial, so they've just let the bastard go free. I want to kill the bastard, but they'll know it was me.'

'What do you want me to do?'

'You've got the connections, Jack, I was hoping that you could sort it out for me.'

'It all costs, Nick, there ain't nothing free in this life.'

'I haven't got much money, but you can have what I have got if you help me out.'

'Well, it might not be money – I might need a favour sometime.'

'Anything, Jack, you just let me know.'

'Right okay, the first thing is that you've got to stay away from this guy for a good while; if anything happens to him in the near future, you'll be the first to be roped in.'

'I know that, that's why I'm here.'

'The next thing is that I need all this guy's details, his name and address, his description. Also we need some distance between you and him when he gets his come-uppance. I'll let you know roughly when it's happening, so that you can make yourself scarce for a while, and find a nice alibi.'

'Sounds okay to me, Jack. I just want him dead.'

'I can understand how you feel at this moment, but you will calm down, and I can see no point in topping the bastard, when a severe warning will be sufficient.'

'What do you mean by a warning?'

'Well it won't be just verbal.'

'I'll leave it with you then, Jack.'

'Good. Let me know when you've got all the details. Here's my home phone number – and don't give it to anyone else.'

'Okay, Jack, message received.'

They both got up and left the office. Jack said goodbye to Nick, then went for a chat to Charles who was outside tinkering with a truck. 'How's business, Charles?'

'It's picking up really well, Jack.'

'Fucking hell, don't let it earn too much, or we'll run out of places to put the money,' Jack laughed.

'I'm sure that you'd find somewhere to put it.'

'You can bet on it, Charles,' Jack laughed. 'Anyway, I'm off for now; you know where I am if you need me.'

'Sure do, Jack.'

Jack got into his car and went home.

'I thought that you were going to ring and let me know when you were coming home, so I could put your tea on,' said Sandra.

'I'm sorry, hon', I forgot, I had other things on my mind.'

'Oh, so I'm that easy to forget, am I?'

'I didn't mean it like that – anyway, do you fancy a takeaway?'

'Sweet-talked your way out of that one didn't you, Dunkerley?' she smiled.

While they were eating their meal, Jack asked Sandra if her uncle Terry still had that piece of land that he'd bought in Portugal some years ago and couldn't get permission to build on it.

'I don't know,' said Sandra. 'I can ring him up and find out.'

Later in the evening, Sandra rang her uncle Terry and asked him if he still owned the land; he said that he did and that he was stuck with it. Jack took the phone from Sandra. 'Hello, Terry, it's Jack here. How much did you pay for it?'

Jack arranged to do a deal with Terry as long as it could all be finalised within two weeks; Terry said that he'd sort it all out and Jack agreed to meet him at his solicitors with the cash when all the papers were ready to be signed.

'What are you up to, Dunkerley?' asked Sandra.

'Not a lot,' replied the grinning Jack.

'First of all you buy a villa in Spain, and now you're buying a chunk of worthless land in Portugal – you're definitely up to something,' she pondered.

'I'll tell you one day, eh, maybe,' he laughed.

One week later Nick rang Jack.

'I've got those details for you, Jack.'

'Right. I'll have to meet you somewhere. I need a chat with you anyway.'

'Should we meet at the pub or at the skip yard?'

'No, I think that it's best if you come over here to my place later, about sevenish.'

'Okay, Jack, I'll be there.'

Nick arrived on time and Jack took him through to his 'office'.

'I've written all the details down that you need – his name, address and what he looks like.'

'Okay, leave it with me.'

'What else did you want to see me about?'

'Do you see much of Slippery Sam these days?'

'Now and again, Jack, why?'

'I want you to go and see him. I want you to beg him to lend you a quarter of a million pounds.'

'Two hundred and fifty grand, Jack! I couldn't get two hundred and fifty pence off that tight bastard.'

'Bear with me while I finish what I'm saying. Tell him you'll give him double the money back in a year; if he doesn't go for that deal then offer him three times the money back. By this time you will have at least got his attention. He'll ask you how safe his money is, and how you can guarantee all what you say; at this point you must swear him to absolute secrecy. By the time he's swore on his life, his children's life and his grandmother's life, you'll know you've got him interested. You then have to appear convinced that you can trust him. You will then tell him that you know of a small company that's for sale, and the company owns a piece of land in Portugal. Go on to tell him that what the owners of the company don't know is that in the next year a new road is going to be built through this land and it's going to be worth millions. Get him interested, Nick, sell the idea to him, then let slip who the English agents are who are dealing with the sale.'

'And what then, Jack?'

'Nothing, you just leave the rest to me.'

Nick spoke to Slippery Sam, but he said that he wasn't interested. A week later the agent rang Jack.

'Hello, Mr Dunkerley, it's Masons here. We seem to have someone interested in your company and the land that you've got for sale with us in Portugal.'

'And what's the name of this chap?'

'It's a Mr Samuel Edwards, do you know him?'

'No,' lied Jack, 'but keep my name out of it anyway. The deal is between the purchaser and my limited company, not me personally.'

'As you wish.'

'Just how interested is he anyway?'

'Oh, he seems quite keen.'

'I'll leave it with you, then,' said Jack as he put down the phone.

Jack then picked up the phone again and rang Frank Crawley.

'Hello, Frank, it's Jack.'

'Hello, Jack. I've not been in touch since that last misadventure because I thought it might not be wise for us to be seen associating together.'

'I know what you mean and it wasn't your fault – the Indian had you over as much as me. Anyway, I need a favour. I want you to use your expertise to bust a company for me, grand style.'

'Shouldn't be a problem, Jack, whose company is it?'

Jack explained the situation to Frank and they worked out between them how they could get the scam to work. Sam Edwards was under the impression that he would have to move fast on the deal, if he wanted to buy the company which owned the land in Portugal before the owners of the company found out its true value. Sam was not really interested in buying the small company, but he would have to buy it as a job lot if he didn't want to arouse any suspicion about the land; just putting an offer in for the land may have made the owners take another look at the deal or even get it revalued, he thought, and he didn't want to chance that; anyway he could always separate the land from the company at a later date, and sell the company on to some unsuspecting mug.

Six weeks later Sam Edwards met up with the English agents in Portugal to look at the land and to sign the deal. Before he would sign any documents, he phoned his own solicitor in England to do a final check on the company that he was buying blind, just to make sure that there were no serious debts that may have suddenly arisen. The answer came back all clear and Sam Edwards signed the documents; then looking at his watch, he put the time and date next to his signature – the time that he wrote was three o'clock. Jack's agent immediately rang Jack as he had been instructed, and told him that the deal was done. Jack thanked him and put the phone down; he then rang Frank.

'Hello, Frank, it's Jack. It's all systems go, the deal's been done, get it sorted.'

'Okay, Jack, everything's ready, I was just waiting for your call.'

'Ring me back later when it's all sorted.'

Jack put the phone back down and looked at his watch; it was now a quarter past two in England. Jack smiled to himself at the thought of Sam Edwards buying a piece of land in Portugal that was worthless; the company that he'd just bought, Cast Iron Holdings Limited, was his old skip company that he'd now bought back, and before three o'clock, with a bit of help from Frank, Cast Iron Holdings Limited would be in debt to the tune of three million pounds.

Frank rang back.

'It's all done, Jack.'

'Cheers, I owe you one.'

'Let's call it straight after that last cock-up, eh?'

'Suits me, Frank.'

And they both put their phones down.

Jack was smiling to himself about the deal; Sam Edwards had paid with a non returnable international money order, so he would never get his money back even if he tried, plus now he was once again lumbered with the skip firm, but this time it was laden with irrecoverable debts. Sam Edwards, so long the devious hunter, was now the prey.

'Funny old world, innit?' Jack mumbled to himself as he wandered into his kitchen to make a cup of tea.

A few days later when Jack and Charles were leaving the skip yard for the last time, a car approached them at speed and the driver slammed on the brakes at the last minute, skidding to a halt close to Jack. An extremely angry Sam Edwards jumped out of the car.

'Which one of you is Jack Dunkerley?' he demanded.

'I am,' said the amused Jack.

'You're the bastard are you? You've left me with nothing.'

'That's not true,' said Jack.

'What do you mean?'

'We've left you the light bulbs, which is more than you left for us when we bought the place from you.'

'Fucking light bulbs, you're a dirty rotten conniving bastard.'

'Get it right, sunshine, dirty rotten conniving *rich* bastard,' Jack grinned.

Sam stepped forward as though to throw a punch at Jack, when Jack said,

'Don't even think about it.'

There was something in Jack's voice that told Sam that he'd better change to a different line of thought. He jumped into his car and as he raced off, he shouted through the car's open window to Jack, 'This isn't over yet.'

'Maybe not,' shouted Jack, 'but it makes me feel pretty good for now.'

Jack and Charles looked at each other and started laughing.

Then they got into their cars and left the skip yard for the final time. The next day Jack called Nick on the telephone.

'Call around to my house sometime today, I've got something for you,' said the mysterious Jack.

Later that day when Nick arrived, Jack gave him an address in Spain.

'This place belongs to a friend of mine. Go and stay there for a couple of weeks. Give me a ring when you get there. Oh, and here's the keys to get in.'

Four days later Nick rang from Spain to let Jack know that he and his wife had arrived.

'Have a nice holiday, Nick,' Jack said as he put the phone down.

Three days later when the child molester was walking home from his local off-licence a mysterious figure stepped from the shadows and shot him in the groin with a sawn-off four ten shotgun; it wasn't enough to kill him, but it was enough to put his ardour into reverse. The molester was unlikely to get an erection ever again; he was now no more of a threat than a neutered tom-cat. One and a half weeks later, Nick was arrested on his return to England, and questioned for some hours by the police. It was just a matter of routine; Nick had a cast-iron alibi and although they suspected that he might have had a hand in it, they had no evidence, and without evidence there was never going to be a case to answer. The day after Nick was released by the police, he called at Jack's house to return the key to the villa and thank him for his help and the nice holiday.

'Tell your friend he's got a nice villa. It's like a palace – my missus loved all that lovely crystal, crystal chandeliers, crystal tables, crystal door knobs, even the bathroom was—'

'Yes, we know,' Jack interrupted.

Sandra caught Jack's eye and gave him a knowing look; Jack winked at her and they both smiled without uttering a word.

Chapter Ten

Mercedes Bents

Another week passed and Jack's phone rang.

'Hello,' said Jack.

'Hello, Jack, it's Saed.'

'Hello, mate, what's happening?'

'Nothing really. I heard that you missed that pair of bastards, Patel and son.'

'Yeah – such is life though, mate. Maybe they'll come back one day, eh?'

'Well if they don't, I'll have their car,' he laughed.

'What car?' asked the now interested Jack.

'They bought a nearly new Mercedes recently, a diesel with the full body kit. They normally ship one out to India every few months.'

'So where is this Merc now?'

'I don't know. It must be in their garage, or the garage of the safe house that I tipped you off about, unless they took it with them.'

'No, that's impossible because they flew, and they were in a hurry.'

'Well, it must still be here, then.'

'Must be, and if it is, it may well be a nice bit of compensation for all the hassle that they've caused me.'

Jack found the car in a lock-up garage at the rear of the Indians' safe house. The documents were in the glove compartment and the keys were on the sun visor – it was as though it was ready to be moved, thought Jack. He took the car home and gave it to Sandra. It was the first item that they had that showed any outward signs of wealth. Jack normally preferred low profile; he'd always said that he'd rather have money than fame – 'you can't eat fame,' he'd said. But on this rare occasion, he made an exception, because it was to be a present for Sandra. There was nothing that he wouldn't do for her; she was that special woman that only comes along once in a lifetime. He had an affinity with her that not even his closest friends and relatives could understand. They all knew Jack and were surprised that he had let anybody enter his world, one that normally had barriers that were impenetrable, but this lady had managed to break them all down with her love for him and he melted in her arms like ice cubes on a summer's day. She was the one he'd been waiting for all of his life, and he was never going to let her go, nor she him. Sandra loved the car with its flash body kit and Jack would tease her by calling her a poseur.

A week and a half later, Jack and Sandra were awoken from their sleep by a bleeping from their house alarm; it was telling them that someone or something was in their garden or drive area. The sensors had detected some form of movement outside – often it would just be a cat or a dog that would set it off. The sensors when activated also turned on the external floodlights. Jack looked out of the window, but could see nothing, then just as he was about to close the curtains and go back to bed, he noticed that the driver's window on Sandra's car had been smashed. Jack went downstairs and into the drive; he took a cricket bat with him for protection against any would-be intruders. He went to the car and saw that someone had also tried to break off the steering lock, but without success. Jack had a good look around for the perpetrator but could find no one.

He went back into the house and got the keys for the Merc, then he moved the car into the garage, which was alarmed.

The next day Sandra telephoned a firm that she had found in the Yellow Pages and they came out to repair the broken window. The car was then drivable, even though the plastic covering around the steering lock was damaged and looked untidy. After a month or so of driving the Mercedes, Sandra complained that it was no cheaper to run than her old Ford.

'It must be,' said Jack, 'it's a diesel.'

'Well, it night be a diesel but it's not any cheaper to run,' complained Sandra.

'I'll get Archie to check it over when he's got the time.'

'Okay, hon',' she said.

Two weeks later, the mechanic Archie arrived at Jack's house to check the vehicle over,

'I can't find any leaks in the pipes or the fuel tank and the engine runs well; maybe you're travelling more miles than you're actually allowing for,' said Archie.

'I'm not going any further in that car than I used to go in my old Ford,' she said adamantly.

'Well try this for an idea – fill the tank up to the top then set your tripmeter; when your fuel level gets to the half way mark, give me a call, and let me know the mileage and I'll work it out for you.'

'Okay,' said Sandra.

A week later when she rang Archie with the mileage, he said, 'That can't be right, are you sure?'

'Yes I'm sure,' she stated quite categorically.

'You'd better bring it to the garage,' said the dumbfounded mechanic.

When the Mercedes was at the garage, he could still find nothing up with it. He changed the filters and gave the car a quick look over; when he checked the tyre pressures, he found them to be nearly double of what they should have been. He let some air out of the tyres until they were at the correct pressure, then he noticed that the tyres then looked flat.

'There's something wrong here,' Archie said to himself. He put the car on the electric ramp and pressed the button for it to go up; he noticed that the ramp was having difficulty lifting the car. He telephoned Jack.

'Listen Jack, you'd better come down here to my garage, there's something funny about this car.'

'I'll be down shortly,' said Jack. 'What's the problem, Archie?'

'Well, Jack, look at the tyres.

'They're all flat.'

'Well, yes and no.'

'What does that mean?'

'Well, it means that they've got the right pressure in them, but they're still flat.'

'So what's the solution?'

'Well, the ramp also had a problem lifting the car, so my figuring is that the car is overweight.'

'What do you mean by overweight?'

'Well I've searched the car without finding anything, so I reckon that there's something hidden in the car somewhere, in the panels, the floor or the chassis.'

'Why haven't you looked?'

'Because it means drilling holes in the car, and I wanted to ask you first.'

'Okay, I'm here, crack on with it.'

'Okay, but any damage is at your expense.'

'Understood, Archie.'

The mechanic drilled some of the internal panels and the floor without success.

'Are you sure that you're not mistaken, Archie? The inside of the car is beginning to resemble a block of gorgonzola cheese.'

'There's something here somewhere. Let's put it back on the ramp.'

Both men watched as the ramp struggled to lift the car. Archie then went under the car and drilled the chassis; when he came out his face was beaming.

'What are you grinning at?' asked Jack.

'Look at this drill bit.'

'What about it?'

'Look at these shavings.'

'Yeah, I can see 'em, but what are they?'

'That's gold, Jack, fucking gold!'

'Bloody 'ell, it is gold, how much of it is in there?'

'Must be quite a bit to make the car that heavy.'

'Looks like I've had a right touch, eh, Archie?'

'Aye, you can say that again.'

'Can you fix the car back up so that nothing is noticeable?'

'No problem at all, Jack.'

'Okay, mate, I'll leave it with you, and don't tell a soul.'

'My lips are sealed.'

Jack left and went to see Pete.

'Pete, I've got a job for you.'

'I'm busy with the gear at the moment, Jack.'

'Well as soon as you've done that, I want you to take Sandra's car to Jersey for a few days.'

Jack explained to Pete about taking the car from the Indians and that a mechanic friend of his had found a stash gold hidden in it.

'That must have been what they were doing, selling their drugs over here, then converting the money into gold, and then shipping the gold to India where it's worth more, so they make money at all ends of the deal,' explained Pete.

'That seems to be the top and bottom of it, Pete,' said the smiling Jack.

'Yeah, you can smile, you jammy bastard.'

'It must be rubbing off you, Pete.'

They both laughed.

Some days later Pete took the ferry to Jersey. Jack had a contact there who rented an old shed in a boatyard to Pete for a few days; when he had got the gold out of the car he telephoned Jack to let him know. Jack then flew to Jersey the next day. Pete collected him from the airport.

'How did it go, Pete?'

'It was a bleedin' struggle, that's how it went.'

'Not to worry, you'll be paid well.'

'Well, there's a godsend,' he laughed.

'I hope that you've hidden it well.'

'Hidden what well?'

'The gold, you loon, what do you think I'm on about?'

'Oh, it's safe all right – it's in the boot.'

'Are you fucking mad, Pete? You've just picked me up at the airport, with God knows how much gold in the boot!'

'What else was I supposed to do with it?'

'Now there's a point,' Jack said nonchalantly.

Pete took Jack to a series of banks where Jack put the gold into safety deposit boxes.

'What good is it in there?' asked Pete.

'Handy for a rainy day,' grinned Jack.

'When will you ever have a rainy day, Jack?'

'One never knows, Pete – I've had some monsoons in the past.'

'Well, if it ever happens again you'll be rich and wet.'

'Well, I've been poor, mate, and I've been reasonably rich, and let me tell you I like rich best.'

They both laughed.

Pete dropped Jack off at the airport and headed for the ferry and the long drive northwards to his home.

At least the fuel bill will be less on the homeward trip, Pete thought. Then again, I'm sure that Jack can afford a few gallons of diesel.

Pete dropped the car off at Jack's house and Sandra came outside to look at her pride and joy.

'Has it been fixed now, Pete?' asked the smiling Sandra.

'Oh it's been fixed all right; it's much lighter to drive now,' he grinned.

'What was the problem?' asked Sandra.

'The previous owner had added some ballast, which kept the car closer to the ground – it's now been taken out.'

'What difference will it make?'

'Well it won't be worth as much, but it runs a lot better.'

Pete and Jack laughed. 'I can't see what's funny,' Sandra complained.

Later that night, when Sandra and the girls were fast asleep, Jack lay awake in bed just thinking things over to himself. He heard a noise from outside his house and got out of bed to peek through the window from behind his curtains. He could see two Asian men trying to get into Sandra's Mercedes; he watched them for a while with some amusement. Jack didn't notice Sandra appear at his side and he was startled when she said, 'What are you looking at?'

'Someone's stealing your car.'

'Someone's stealing my car and you're standing there watching them?' she started to scream at him.

Jack put his hand over her mouth.

'Shush, honey, I know what I'm doing. I'll buy you another car, two if you like.'

He took his hand from her mouth and she watched in disbelief as the two men drove away in her car.

'I'll explain it all to you one day, honey, I promise.'

'I'm not sure if I want to know,' she said.

'Let's get back into bed, we've got a long day tomorrow, and we've got to find you another car,' said Jack.

'I hope so, Jack, or I'll have to borrow yours,' she giggled.

'It'd be like cutting my legs off,' said Jack.

'Now there's an idea,' she reasoned, 'then I could keep you in bed, twenty-four hours a day.' She laughed as she put her arms around him.

Chapter Eleven

What Goes Around Comes Around

Jack relaxed in his armchair reading the local newspaper; he'd read most of it and was just flipping through the last pages when a picture caught his eye. A photograph of a man on the page leapt out at him; it was a man being presented with a long service medal on his retirement. Jack lingered on the page, just staring at the face of the man who he had hated for so long. The haunting face of Inspector Graylor stared back at him from the page. Now, thought Jack, at last this horrible bastard was about to lose the shield that he had hidden behind for so long, the protection of being in the police force. Jack took note of the date when the inspector would be officially retiring. The following day he drove into town and used a telephone box.

'Hello, Max.'

'Jack, how are you?'

'I'm fine, and you?'

'Yeah, me too.'

'When can we meet? I've got a job for you.'

'Good, as soon as possible, I need the money.'

The following week Jack and Max met for the first time since Max had done the Spanish job. Max was looking forward to another prosperous arrangement. Jack explained to him that this time it was purely personal and that he wanted this to be absolutely watertight.

'No loose ends on this one, Max.'

'I never leave loose ends,' said the now insulted Max.

'No, I didn't mean that you did. What I'm saying is that especially in this case, we can't afford any loose ends – we don't want the odd-lot crawling all over us, do we?'

'Leave it with me, Jack, I'll come up with something; just give me all his details and I'll let you know when something happens.'

Max went away to study his next target. This one, he thought, will not be easy, but also it will not be impossible; everything and anything is possible, thought Max, as he browsed over the inspector's details and the cutting from the newspaper with such a clear photograph of the almost-retired Inspector Graylor. It was to be four weeks later when the inspector officially retired, and Jack had some news for Max.

'Hello, Max, it's Jack, listen to this, I've heard a strong rumour that our inspector friend is taking his wife abroad on holiday soon after he retires. I don't know where or when, that's your department – I'll leave it with you.'

'Okay, Jack, I'm on it.'

The conversation finished and both of them returned to different tasks; Jack to the business in hand with Pete and Max to follow up the tip that Jack had given to him.

Six weeks later the inspector and his wife landed at Malta's Luqa Airport for a month's holiday to celebrate his retirement. A taxi took them to the Holiday Inn, in the centre of town. The inspector's wife was already having difficulty coping with the humidity and the heat of this Mediterranean island, where the days were typically tropical and the nights dropped to what felt like freezing point; she would not acclimatise easily. After the first couple of days and nights of constantly being awake, the inspector's wife adopted the method of tiring herself during the day, and going to bed early in the evenings, leaving the inspector to drink the nights away at the hotel bar, until he staggered into her bedroom in the early hours, somewhat worse for wear.

One evening the inspector got talking to an Englishman who was also a guest at the hotel. They drank and talked into the small hours; the inspector bragged about his thirty years' service in the police force, and how he'd come to Malta to give his wife a treat, although he hadn't really wanted to go further than Torquay himself. The inspector was as drunk as a lord.

'Thirty years of service, that's what I give 'em, thirty years of my life, then they just toss me on the scrap heap. Bastards, bastards, bastards!'

'It's a cruel world,' said his drinking partner.

'Yep, sure is, but they're still bastards,' said the inebriated inspector.

His new-found friend walked him to his room.

'I'll see you in the bar tomorrow,' rambled the inspector.

'Maybe,' said his friend.

The next evening after a few drinks, the inspector's new friend offered to take him to a different bar for a change.

'Lead the way,' said the inspector.

The inspector followed his new friend to a club just a few hundred yards away from their hotel, where the scantily clad dancers and hostesses seemed to tantalise the taste buds of the previously aloof inspector. After a few more drinks the inspector was completely without inhibitions; he allowed the dancers to drag him around the room, while he did a drunken version of the waltz. Later, one of the hostesses led the inspector to a private room where they had sex, the inspector unaware that his friend had paid the girl. The smiling, drunken inspector resurfaced some time later and kept rambling to his friend, 'You won't tell my wife, will you, my friend?'

'Not a chance of it.'

'You're sure, you won't tell her?'

'I'm positive.'

'Cross your heart and hope to die,' grinned the drunken inspector.

'Yes, yes, yes, anything. Come on, it's time that we got back before she notices you missing.'

'It'll be all right, I'll slip in quietly.'

The man walked Graylor back to his room and agreed to meet him the next night in the bar; they had become drinking buddies. The next night in the bar, the two men were discussing war and the different wars around the world and the unofficial things that soldiers do during conflicts. 'In the troubles of Ireland, the soldiers had picked up people that they suspected of the slightest offence in the street and psychologically tortured them for hours,' said the inspector.

'In the Falklands some of the soldiers had cut off the ears of any of the enemies that they had shot and kept them as mementoes – some of them had a string of ears hanging from their belts,' said the other.

'Never!' said the inspector adamantly.

'Oh it's true,' said the other. 'I know, because I was there.'

'My God, were you really?'

'Yes, my friend, really.'

They wandered onto the topic and the never-ending stories of Vietnam, and the things that the GIs used to do to relieve the monotony of their long tours of duty. One of the things mentioned was the incredibly dangerous game of Russian roulette.

'Surely they never really used to play it?' said the inspector. 'But of course they did, it was a big money earner. They used to take bets on it.'

'Surely not,' said the inspector as he finished another in a long session of drinks.

'I'm afraid it's true, but it's not that dangerous.'

'Not that dangerous, not that bloody dangerous, are you mad?' exclaimed the inspector.

'Not mad, just logical, it's easily explained.'

'Tell me then.'

'I'll tell you tomorrow.'

'Why not now?'

'Tomorrow will reveal all, okay?'

'Yes okay.'

And on that note the inspector staggered off to find his bed. The following night in the bar, the inspector's drinking partner pulled out a revolver. 'What are you doing with that?'

'I'm going to show you the trick.'

'Put it away, you'll get arrested.'

'Always the policeman, eh? In this country it's not such a big deal.'

'Are you sure?'

'Oh I'm sure.'

'Well, go on then, explain the illusion, if there is one.'

The man explained how the cylinder of the gun was oiled well so that it spun freely. He then went on to explain how the gunpowder was taken out of the bullet and replaced by more lead, making it even heavier, thus explaining why it was that every time the bullet was put in the cylinder and rotated, the weight of the bullet, with a bit of help from gravity, always brought the bullet to the lower end of the chamber, eluding the firing pin; even if the firing pin did connect, there was no chance of any mishap because the bullet had been doctored in such a way that it was incapable of being fired.

'I'm impressed,' said the inspector.

'Would you like to try it?'

'Not for me, thanks, I'm more the spectator type.'

The other spun the cylinder of the weapon, put the gun to his head and pulled the trigger. He did it several times, and then offered the gun to the half-drunk inspector, who, although he was hesitant, did not wish to appear to be a coward. He took the weapon from the table, rotated the cylinder, then held the gun to the side of his head for a while, breaking out into a sweat before finally squeezing the trigger. On realisation that he was alive, he had another go, then another, and another, feeling quite pleased with himself.

'Now do you believe me?' said his friend.

'I do now.'

They had more drinks and continued to discuss the game of Russian roulette. The inspector was now happy with the knowledge that the game was fixed so that no player ever really risked his life. The quite drunken pair went on to the club where they had been the night before, where the inspector had danced with the dancers and toyed with the hostess. When they got into the club they were given a table in a prime position to watch the floor show. The inspector, in a drunken state, gathered a crowd around his table, and with the inspector leading the crowd on, they goaded his friend into showing them his party piece, the ultimate game of death, Russian roulette. They both knew it was a scam but the ever-increasing audience did not. He rotated the cylinder of the weapon and put the barrel to his head, and then as the cylinder came to rest he pulled the trigger, to loud gasps then huge applause from the audience. 'Encore, encore,' they shouted while applauding what they assumed was a courageous act. Once again he rotated the cylinder and put the barrel to his head, pulling the trigger once more, to the thrill of his audience.

The inspector, sensing that his drinking partner was getting all the glory and that there was no real risk involved in the act, took the weapon from his partner and copied the same procedures as the latter had done, repeating the act several times to the astonishment of his new-found friends and audience. 'Bravo bravo!' they shouted at him, feeding his already over-inflated ego. He put the weapon down on the table, stood on a chair and bowed to the crowd, who cheered and applauded him, before the hostess with whom he'd had sex on the previous occasion came over and sat with him for a while before leading him to her private room, again courtesy of his friend who was paying her bill. The inspector's friend fiddled with the gun for a while then put it back on the table. Later, when the inspector returned, he picked up the gun from the table, rotated the cylinder, then fired it at the head of his friend, much to his own delight and much to the horror of his friend who broke out into a sweat.

'Just messing pal, just messing,' the inspector said.

He rotated the cylinder once more and put the barrel to his own head, then pulled the trigger while laughing in a drunken manner. He then put the gun back on the table as the hostess approached him. She sat on his knee and kissed him, then picked up the weapon from the table, rotated the cylinder and put it to her own head, but the inspector took it from her, spun the cylinder once more while putting the barrel to his head, and laughed out loudly as he pulled the trigger, splattering blood all over the hostess as he blew his own brains out in front of many onlookers. The place was in uproar as people ran around screaming and shouting for an ambulance.

Max knew it was too late for an ambulance as he walked past the crowd to the outside of the building to dispose of the weighted bullet that he had exchanged earlier for a real one while the inspector was busy having sex with the hostess, paid for once again by Max.

Chapter Twelve

Burning Ambition

'I've got to nip out to see our Charles,' Jack said. 'Do you fancy coming with me, Sandra?'

'No, you go, Jack, I've got to be at the doctor's at three o'clock.'

'Why, are you ill or something?'

'Something maybe, but it's just women's stuff, Jack, nothing to interest you.

'Okay, I'll see you later, then.'

Jack returned at teatime to find Sandra cooking him a meal. 'Everything all right at the doctor's, hon'?'

'Yes, love, everything's just fine,' she smiled.

'It's time that we got away from here, San.'

'A nice break would be welcome,' she answered.

'I need more than a short break to sort my arthritis out,' moaned Jack.

The next day when Jack picked up his newspaper, the headline that caught his eye brought him a feeling of satisfaction: EX-POLICE OFFICER COMMITS SUICIDE ON SUNSHINE ISLE. Jack went on to read the story of Inspector Graylor and the mysterious events surrounding his death; the mention of Russian roulette had captured the imagination of the tabloid press and its readers. There was lots of speculation as to the reasons why an ex-inspector of police should commit suicide at the beginning of the end of his working life, and still only fifty years old. Some of his old colleagues gave their opinions – 'I can't believe he's done it,' said one. 'He had a good pension and plenty of time to spend it,' said another. 'It all seems very odd.'

A lot odder than they realise, thought Jack as a wry smile crossed his face at the thought of the ever-present thorn in his side being pruned at last.

Jack didn't fancy the idea of retiring but Sandra was forever trying to talk him into it, and the pressure of the type of business that he was in was taking its toll; that plus the arthritic shoulder and the fact that he had enough money to last him for two lifetimes brought the possibility of retiring to the forefront of his mind.

Jack went to see each of his buyers individually. He also had the same discussion with Pete.

'It is now time to pack the business in and get out while we're ahead,' Jack told them. 'We've all had a good run and earned a tidy living, so let's not push our luck any further.'

He explained that he planned to retire, but before he did anything drastic, he would help any of them that needed assistance to organise their money into safe investments that would give them good returns, so that they would never have to worry about money again. Over the next two weeks, Jack met up with each of the men and explained to each of them that he personally was going to split his own money into three parts; one third would stay in an off shore company account, another third would go into BDDI, an Anglo-Asian bank that paid high interest rates, and the final third would go into a firm that dealt in government bonds and gilts. 'This way I won't have to worry about losing my money or having it seized by the odd-lot,' he told them. Each of the men agreed to follow suit with Jack's plan and Jack made the arrangements for them all to transfer monies to the relevant places.

'Well, San, only another few months and we're in the millennium,' said Jack.

'Where would you like to celebrate the turn of the century, honey?'

'Maybe we could go to London to see the sights and then go to Trafalgar Square for the midnight celebrations!'

'Bleedin' London!' said Jack. 'I was thinking more like Sydney in Australia. We could celebrate in the sunshine, not standing in Trafalgar Square in the freezing cold, weighted down by a big overcoat and a woolly scarf.'

'I don't think we'll be going to Australia somehow, Jack.'

'Whyever not, Sandra? It's only a few hours away by aeroplane.'

'That's the problem.'

'What's the problem?' asked Jack.

'Flying, Jack.'

'Is this some sort of enigma Sandra? What's the problem with flying?'

'Do you remember when I went to the doctor's?'

'Yes, but what's that got to do with flying? Are you ill?'

'Not really, but by the time the New Year celebrations begin, I'll be noticeably pregnant,' she grinned.

'But you can't be!' said the shocked Jack.

'Oh, but I am.'

'Are you sure?'

'Surely, definitely, positive.'

'Well, why didn't you tell me before?'

'I was waiting for the right moment.'

'Is there ever one?'

'Apparently not,' said the giggling Sandra.

'I'll be forty-five next year,' said Jack, still in shock.

'And I'll be thirty-five,' said Sandra, 'but you'll also be retired, so we'll all have more time to spend as a family.'

'Now there's a point,' mused Jack as the reality of what Sandra had just told him began to unfold. His temporarily clouded thoughts started to clear, and visions of his long awaited son now became a possibility.

Some weeks later, at three in the morning when all was silent and the perpetrators were hidden by darkness of night, the two Asian men who had stolen Sandra's Mercedes sneaked up the drive once more. This time they stopped outside the front door of the house. One of the men was carrying a fuel can and the other carried a bicycle pump. One of the men took the top off the fuel can, and the other one immediately began to draw fuel from the can with the pump; he was drawing fuel from the can and squirting it through the now propped-open letter box into the hallway of the house. After some minutes of this activity one of the men pulled a rag from his pocket and put half of it through the letter box leaving the other half dangling on the outside of the house; then the man lit the rag and both men ran away from the house. The two men waited in the distance, watching the house until they could see flames blazing high, cutting eerily through the night's darkness like a witch's bonfire on Halloween.

Jack rolled over in his bed, dripping with sweat in the heat; still asleep, he kicked off the top sheet, now not able to get comfortable and sweating profusely. He opened his eyes, and then rolled himself out of the bed and staggered towards the door, feeling about in the darkness for the door handle. As he felt along the panel of the door he felt in his hand the crystal door knob which he turned, and on opening the door he stepped out onto the balcony and into the warm night air of Spain.

Sandra noticed that Jack was missing. 'Where are you, Jack?' she shouted softly.

'I'm only here, honey,' he replied.

Sandra, also sweating in the night's heat, left her bed and stood with Jack on the balcony of their villa.

'It's too hot for me to sleep, honey,' she said.

'It'll be all right tomorrow, honey, I'll get someone out to fix the air-conditioning.'

'Can't they come now?'

'I doubt it, hon'.'

'I almost wish that I was in our old house again back in England.'

'We can't have everything, honey, and we couldn't stay there with Slippery Sam's solicitor harassing us; after all, the house does belong to Cast Iron Holdings Limited.'